Other Helen Reardon Novels

Strands Across the Sea

Man of Vision

Dual Footsteps in the Fog

A Long Time Dead

A story inspired by the search
for a grandfather

**Copyright 2013
Helen Reardon**

ISBN 978-0473253394

Prologue

It was a night like any other. After 10 hours working at the mill what else was there to do but go to the Imperial Hotel and share a few drinks with your workmates? The liquor flowed and the crowd was boisterous. They knew he was an entertainer and could sing many a ballad. A song from the old land. A tune from far away Scotland. They cheered as he performed and refilled his glass. They were men of the soil, brought here to people an empty land. And when their dreams evaporated they were drawn to this desolate little town where the saw mill would pay them a steady wage.

Then some would return to their wives and children and buy their own land. That was the dream and the songs were a reminder of lost ideals and hope unfulfilled.

But now they were being sent out onto the road. Time to go, said the publican who was ready to retire for the night. So they wandered out to their huts and boarding houses. But he was not ready to go back to his room to spend another night alone with his thoughts about Mary.

She was waiting for him as he felled the mighty timber and saved a few precious pounds to return to her and buy them their dream.

He staggered out into the night air and lurched along the street towards the park on the corner with its trees and benches. The bottle of whisky in his coat pocket would ward off the cold. His thoughts returned to Mary. He sat on the bench and the moon went down behind a cloud. He coughed and pulled his shabby coat tighter around his lean frame. He drained the bottle and closed his eyes to dream of better things. And then he fell asleep, the cold night air closing in around him.

Chapter 1

The grassy plot was neatly mown, surrounded by weathered headstones over a century old. But no monument marked this grave site. Not even a simple wooden cross. Whose remains were buried there beneath the earth, five feet down?

"Who knows and who really cares?" Alana Cooper sighed as she put down her notebook and camera and contemplated the grassy mound. Recording the inscriptions on gravestones was an interesting project at times, but more often than not, a frustrating one.

Especially in the older section of the small country cemetery, where many of the stones were unreadable, with rusted iron rails and broken concrete slabs the only memorials to a person or family who had lived in this former timber town.

Alana marked off the site on her cemetery map and moved on to the next plot. The identity of the unmarked grave would be solved back at her lodgings where she kept a copy of the burial records.

She glanced at her watch and saw it was almost time for lunch. She would grab a sandwich and coffee at the town's café and then drive back to the city for her appointment with the museum committee that was funding the project. A degree in sociology didn't always guarantee employment and with a student loan to repay, she was lucky to find this temporary job.

As Alana entered the café, she was conscious of several eyes turned in her direction. The small inland town of Springvale was about five kilometres off the main highway, and the café, with its country kitchen theme, attracted few tourists as most took the main road or scenic route along the coastline to Wellington.

The logging industry had long since disappeared and dairy farming had taken its place, so Kirsty's Kitchen was now a meeting place for farmers' wives during their weekly shopping trip to town or farmhands with an hour or two to spare between milking. Alana, although dressed casually in jeans and a rather shapeless sweater, was a welcome distraction.

Alana helped herself to a wrapped salad and ham sandwich and ordered coffee, then chose a seat near the window where she could look out onto the quiet street with its typical selection of small-town stores with verandahs and 1900's facades painted in a range of bright colours. A chemist shop and hardware store, then book store and law office stood in a row, in defiance of the new shopping centre on the highway.

Glancing at her notebook, Alana was happy with her progress so far. This was her first week in Springvale where she was staying at the roadside tavern. She would be pleased to get back to her small hillside apartment in the city tonight where she would spend the weekend and catch up with her friend, Angela. She had already completed about one third of the cemetery project, photographing and noting the wording on the headstones, then filling in the missing names from the cemetery register.

She thought about the most recent entry, Block 4, Plot 6, Grave 24, and wondered again about the identity of the body buried below. A smooth grassy mound with no markings, undisturbed for almost 100 years. She knew she would have to find the answer at the first opportunity.

Her meeting was at Wellington's maritime museum on the harbour's edge and it was after three o'clock before she pulled into the parking area in front. She had found the time to shower and change her clothes back at the apartment and with the results of her first week's work in a satchel, she felt confident as she entered the building.

She didn't have long to wait before the committee members who were running the cemetery project arrived, anxious to hear how her work was progressing. Estelle Jones was a tall handsome woman in her late sixties who worked part-time at the museum and Jonathan Wilson was a short balding man about the same age, with a long-time interest in historical events in the city.

"So, you seem to be getting through the work very well," said Jonathan as they sat in the small crowded office near the reception desk. "We were so pleased to get the funding for this project which will be of great interest to family researchers."

"Yes, it sure beats looking through files full of microfiche in the back room of a library," Estelle added with a smile. She was balancing a cup of coffee on her lap as she flicked through the pages of notes which Alana had printed out. "Once these names are on the Internet, families will be able to send us more details and their history can be preserved."

Alana was pleased with their reaction to her work. If this project was successful it could lead to more employment. She watched as Jonathan placed the camera chip into the computer and the headstones and unmarked plots were revealed on the screen.

"A tidy cemetery it seems but many of the older graves need attention." Jonathan was looking closely at the photographs. "Once we match the photographs with the names and descriptions we will have a better picture of the residents who lived in the town."

"Many of these older graves would be men who worked at the timber mill and their families." Alana was studying the photographs closely. "There are probably whole families buried in some plots."

The last photograph of all showed the grass-covered mound in lonely contrast to the other graves. "I wonder what the story is here." Estelle's curiosity was aroused. "It would be interesting to know what sort of person has no adornment on his grave. Maybe a foreign mill-hand with no family connections or friends to say goodbye."

As arranged, Alana left the printed copies and photographs with the committee members, who would help with the deciphering of the words on the headstones. She would be kept busy enough identifying the unmarked graves.

Once outside, she decided to walk for a time on the pier, admiring the boats alongside the wharf and watching as the Inter Island ferry came into view. Wellington was a beautiful city when the sun was shining and she was happy to be living here.

But now it was time to forget work for a while and catch up with her friend Angela who had been anxiously texting to see whether she was back in town. Angela had also completed a degree, but had majored in architecture. Historic buildings, rather than gravestones were her specialty.

By the time she had sent Angela a message, the sun was going down and the air was much cooler. Yes, they would meet at an Irish bar in Cuba Street, where they would enjoy a handle of Irish beer and a bowl of their famous chowder.

Meeting with a girl friend was about as much of a social life as Alana had allowed herself. The four years of study, plus working evenings at a grocery store stacking shelves, was not exactly conducive to finding a romantic partner. No, there was plenty of time for that later when she had completed her studies and found a well paying job.

The evening went very much as she expected. They sat in a small booth with a rough wooden table and photographs of Irish whiskey on the walls. Angela was full of her latest news about the preservation of the houses in the fashionable suburb of Oriental Bay. Her family had once owned a number of these dwellings and she claimed that her great grandfather had saved the beach from becoming a boat harbour.

"He lived right on the beachfront and set up a petition that everyone signed. The beach was saved and the shipyard moved further around the waterfront," she said. "I wish I owned just one of those houses now, especially one that has recently been restored. It's strange how family fortunes come and go."

Alana smiled. She had heard the story before. There were riches to rags stories in her family too, but that was now of historic interest only. She would like to have shared the story of the lonely plot at the small cemetery in Springvale but knew that Angela would not share her fascination.

By the time she reached her apartment on the hillside she was ready for bed and a good night's sleep. It was about 2am when she woke suddenly. Her dreams had been disturbed. A Scotsman in a kilt seemed to be beckoning her. He was leading her to a mound of earth, neatly mown, with no stone or cross to identify it. Something was stirring five feet under the ground.

She realised she was sweating so she pulled the covers aside. Her week's work in the graveyard was getting to her. She needed to find the identity of the person buried in that lonely plot as soon as possible. She would go back to Springvale some time over the weekend and not wait for Monday morning as she had previously planned. With that resolve she turned over and drifted back into a dreamless sleep.

Chapter 2

Saturday turned out cool and damp so Alana was happy to spend the day in her apartment catching up on a few chores and attempting to dry her washing. She couldn't afford the luxury of a clothes dryer so garments hung over a drying rack in front of the big bay window.

She called her mother who lived alone in Taupo, where the family had farmed for many years before her father, Ben Cooper, died of a heart attack two years ago. Margaret Cooper now lived in a small block of town houses overlooking the lake and mountains and was anxious to hear news of Alana's first week in Springvale.

"It sounds like a dreary little town to me, my dear. You'll be pleased to get the project done and be back in the city. You must come and spend some time with me as soon as you can and catch up with your old school friends."

Alana smiled as she answered. She had lived near Taupo for much of her teenage years and knew the local crowd. Many had also left for study in the larger centres or gone away on the big 'overseas' experience' that New Zealanders were famous for.

"Actually, the time is going very fast in Springvale. I've hardly had a chance to do anything but photograph graves and eat and sleep." Her mother didn't sound convinced. "Life's too short to hide yourself away. You had enough of that when we were tied to the farm. Thank goodness it wasn't dairying or we would have been stuck there more than we were."

Margaret Cooper had never really adapted to country life and had always found an excuse to travel to the northern city of Auckland or south to Wellington whenever she could manage it. Although she missed her daughter, she was pleased that Alana had chosen Wellington for her university studies.

Alana's brother Sandy had stayed in Taupo, however, and taken over the farm when their father died. His wife, Joanne, had adapted well to farming life and somehow managed to combine rural life with part-time teaching at the local school.

Talking to her mother made Alana feel restless. She didn't miss Taupo and the farm but she sometimes missed her friends, particularly in the winter months when they'd travel to the mountains for a day of skiing or snowboarding.

Donning a light jacket, she set off down the narrow pathway that led to the street below and onto the pavement. Wellington was known for its steep hillsides and turn-of-the century houses clinging to the ledges. She could easily walk to the grocery store so rarely used her car unless she was travelling away from the city.

Half an hour later she was back with the ingredients for a pasta meal and a bottle of wine. Her friend Angela was away visiting family so she would spend the rest of the day alone, reading and watching sport on television.

But the Springvale graveyard kept coming into her mind. She had already loaded the photographs into her computer and couldn't resist going back to review the results. Each image was labeled with its number which corresponded to the cemetery plan.

Many of the graves had no headstones and several were unreadable, but there was something different about Grave 24 in Plot 6. Not a sign of anything but a grass-covered mound of earth.

14

✳✳✳✳✳✳✳✳✳✳✳✳✳✳✳✳

Sunday morning dawned fine but windy and with nothing to keep her in Wellington, Alana left just before noon to return to Springvale. Her room at the tavern was being paid for by the museum project and she was able to come and go as she pleased. Her hosts were a couple in their sixties who had retired from farming and now ran the country pub.

"You're back early Alana. Couldn't keep away from the excitement of Springvale I see." Bruce and Jan Evans were pleased to see her back. Most of their trade came from herd testers and farm machinery salespeople who would stay a night and then move on. It was unusual to have a guest who would be here for a month.

"Yes, back to the graveyard for some company," Alana replied. "There wasn't much doing in the city this weekend." The Evans laughed. They knew that Wellington offered a wide variety of entertainment, from shows and concerts to movies and sports events, but realised that many of these were probably outside a student's budget.

"We'll expect you back for dinner then. There are a number of bookings already. " Jan enjoyed catering for her guests and the locals who came in for an occasional night out, while Bruce was more comfortable pouring drinks behind the bar.

Alana walked to the cemetery, just a few hundred metres away. There had been a burial since she was last here and the new grave was piled high with earth. Flowers overflowed onto the path between the gravesites and momentoes had been left there. A beer bottle, leather

15

jacket, a stuffed toy. This young man was mourned and would be remembered.

Grave 24 looked much the same as before, or had the grass grown a little greener, and surely the dandelion plant with its bright yellow flowers hadn't been there two days ago. Alana was letting her imagination run away with her. But an insistent bee buzzed over the site, landed on the flower and then circled in the air.

There was nothing more she could do here today, so Alana walked back through the village. All the shops were closed apart from the café where a few teenagers gathered. Back at the tavern she would look up the cemetery listing and solve the mystery. Soon she would know who lay beneath that mound of earth.

****

She could smell the food cooking as she entered the lobby of the tavern. There would be a choice of roast beef or lamb, a chicken dish and something vegetarian she was sure. It was a simple menu but the food was well cooked and saved her the trouble of cooking for herself. There were two couples in the dining room already and a group sitting beside the bar.

As there was company, Alana went upstairs to her room to change into something tidier. A clean pair of jeans and a red shirt would suffice. It was always a little strange sitting alone in a hotel dining room but she sat at a corner table and ordered a white wine which came with a plate of corn chips and salsa. She could observe the rest of the diners from here and not feel too conspicuous. She noticed a copy of the morning paper on a table and scanned the front page.

16

Then Jan Evans was beside her to take her order. "I strongly recommend the roast beef tonight love. It comes with all the trimmings and there's a lovely apple pie to follow." Alana was usually a pasta and noodles kind of person but thought it would be a reminder of life back home on the farm where the Sunday roast was a tradition.

The meal was delicious but she was impatient to get back to her room to check out the cemetery website and the details it provided. She punched in the graveyard and the plot and waited anxiously. And then the name came up. August 30, 1912. John Stirling Cameron, age 35. No headstone.

There must be someone still alive in this small community who would remember this man. How did he die? Why was there no headstone, not even a simple cross to bear his name? But she could search further into the old newspaper records. Some were on line and others held at the local museums. There would be many John Camerons, of that she was sure, but the middle name Stirling might provide more clues.

****

Otago 1910

It was a lovely day for a wedding. The early morning sun shone through the misty clouds which would lift as the temperature rose. By lunch-time it would be a perfect South Island day.

Florence Matthews was all of a dither. The guests would begin to arrive soon and her young niece Mary, who was to be her attendant, was nowhere to be seen. As Florence looked out the casement window of the farmhouse and down onto the garden below she could see the seating arranged in the garden and the tent where the food would be served.

She hadn't laid eyes on Walter, her husband-to-be, as was the custom on a bride's wedding day, but John Cameron, Walter's best friend had been on hand all morning to help with the arrangements. She had to admit he was a handsome fellow with his dark good looks and muscular frame.

As well as working with Walter in the newspaper office, John ran a bath house and fitness studio and trained a team of weightlifters who were keenly working towards a competition to be held in the nearby city of Dunedin.

Yes, Walter and John had been friends, and confirmed bachelors, for many a year. But recently Walter had changed his mind and proposed marriage to Florence, who at 32 years of age was beginning to think she was to be left 'on the shelf'.

The sound of laughter drew her attention to the summer house in the corner of the garden, where roses bloomed over the trellis frame. She recognised John Cameron and a female who ran back along the path towards the house, her long skirt caught up under her arm.

Surely it couldn't be young Mary, who was barely 18, alone in the summer house with John who was twice her age. Florence turned away from the window and sat on a stool in front of the mirror above her dressing table. What scandalous behaviour on her wedding day. She would have to talk to Mary's mother about her precocious daughter.

But soon Mary came into the room, her usually pale cheeks rosy and her eyes bright. Florence did not speak, but continued to brush her hair and Mary began to chat about the day ahead.

"You should see the flower arrangements in the hall, and the caterers are busy re-arranging your sister's kitchen. This is so exciting. I can hardly wait for my own wedding day." Mary picked up a comb and began to fashion Florence's hair into a stylish knot.

Their dresses lay on the over-stuffed bed and Florence was already wearing her new undergarments under a silk robe. Florence had chosen a dress of heavy brocade in pale blue, nipped in at the waist, with a tiered skirt, long sleeves and a crocheted collar.

Mary's dress was similar in style but made from a softer material in red, also adorned with a wide collar. Their wide-brimmed hats were swathed in chiffon with artificial flowers tucked under the brim.

Florence had to smile at Mary's enthusiasm and felt a tingle of excitement at what lay ahead. By the end of the day she would be Walter's wife and they would be taking the train to the city of Dunedin for their four-day honeymoon.

19

＊＊＊＊＊＊＊＊＊＊＊

Cool, damp weather on Monday morning meant photographing graves was out of the question. Alana decided to catch up with her reports and then try to locate some-one who might answer some of her questions about John Stirling Cameron. The old saw mill had closed many years ago when the dairy boom took over, but there could still be people living in the area who remembered some of its stories.

The local paper was always a good place to start. The Tribune had been published for many years but would the office hold records dating back to the early 1900s? There was only one way to find out and soon Alana was questioning the young girl behind the reception desk. "All the old papers went to the museum as far as I know," she said. "That was when they moved office about five years before my time."

Like most small museums, the Springvale Pioneer Museum was run by volunteers and only open a few hours each week. There was a contact number beside the door, however, and soon Alana was talking to Flo Avery, the museum curator. Yes, she would open up the museum for Alana and help her with any information about the old milling days in the area. Timber milling had been the area's life blood in the late 1800s and early 1900s when the native forests were felled and replanted with pine.

As Alana walked into the rear entrance of the small museum the past was all around her. A display of old farm equipment and a laundry with washing machines and tin tubs made way for a doll collection and technology bay with typewriters and vacuum cleaners. There were so many objects on display it was impossible to take it all in and Alana smiled as she compared it to the city museums with their pristine displays and elaborate signage.

"I'm sorry it is all a bit of a clutter," Flo Avery apologized. "We are quite short handed at present with several members ill and one who has passed on over the holiday break." Alana looked around, appreciating the variety of items before her eyes, knowing that over the years the original families living in the area had donated them to the collection.

Following Flo into the small office she found space on a chair beside the cluttered desk and began to explain the reason for her visit. She soon learned that there was a great deal of information available about the early sawmilling days, mostly newspaper cuttings kept in old scrapbooks as well as folders bulging with notes and photos.

There was a work table in an upstairs area and this is where Alana spent the next two hours, browsing through the notes and photographs. She was given the use of an ancient photocopier and had soon copied several of the pages that told the story of the small town which was established in 1880 in the densely forested area which stretched over more than 40 miles.

At first Springvale had been a timber town but once the bush was cleared it became a service centre for the sheep and dairy farms which were gradually established in the area. A number of sawmills were working in the early days with timber being transported by rail to the nearby city for building construction. One of the largest mills was close to the river which ran beside the small settlement of Springvale and according to a newspaper article, the remnants of the workings were still visible.

Many of the workers lived in one of the three hotels or in boarding houses which were run by wives of the workers to bring in extra funds during the depression years. Others lived in the small wooden huts at the mill on the outskirts of the town.

Just as Alana was about to pack up and head back to the hotel room, Flo Avery came up the stairs clutching another folder. "I've found this old wages book with the names of many of the mill workers," she said. "Let's see if we can find some mention of your John Cameron." The names and figures had been laboriously hand written and starting with the pages for 1910, Alana ran her eyes down the list. Nothing there.

It wasn't until she reached the columns for May 1912 that the first listing for John Cameron came up. He was listed as a mill hand, earning two pounds seven and sixpence. From there the name appeared each week until August 30 and then a short note. Deceased. No known family.

Chapter 3

After spending the morning at the museum Alana walked back to the tavern and set the pile of papers down on the small table in the corner of the room. She sat and leafed through them building up a picture in her mind of the town in its hey day with the busy mill and hundreds of workers from all around the world.

She stood and looked out to the street where the men had bought their goods and met in the saloons and bars of the hotels. There would have been plenty of talk and laughter as they relaxed after a long day in the mill or out in the forest. She looked again at the death record for John Stirling Cameron. Mill hand, formerly journalist. Circumstances must have been tough to send an educated man like that to such a harsh environment.

With this on her mind, Alana picked up her bag and set off to buy some lunch. The weather had cleared, so she planned to sit in the park beside the stream with a sandwich and then return to the graveyard where there was so much more work to be done. She was only part way through the project and time was precious. The afternoon passed quickly and by the end of the day, Alana had photographed a further section of graves and noted down the inscriptions which were difficult to read. She knew the monuments which were well maintained would present no problem as the photographs would tell the story.

There was time to transfer her notes to the laptop computer before dinner so she set about the task before changing into clean jeans and a tidy blouse and heading for the dining room. Tonight there was a group of young farmers enjoying a dinner meeting and the tables were almost all taken. As Bruce Evans poured her a glass of white wine, Alana perched on a bar stool and looked around for a place to sit. "Try the seat by the window," Bruce suggested. "It's as good a place as any." With a smile Alana picked up her glass and walked towards the table just as a tall dark-haired man headed for the same place.

"Oh, I'm sorry. I didn't know this table was taken," he said. He stood and looked around the room and then smiled at Alana. "Do you mind sharing this table? It looks as though the inn is full tonight." "Not at all," Alana answered. She usually preferred her own company but the young man seemed pleasant enough. She studied the menu and decided on the pasta dish with salad, then returned the menu to the table and took a sip of her wine.

"That was a quick decision. I haven't eaten here for a while so what do you recommend?" Alana was soon pointing out the dishes she had tried and by the time Jan Evans came to take their order, the two of them were chatting about their favourite foods and wine. "Let me introduce you," Jan said with a twinkle in her eye. "Alana, this is Jason Black who has stayed with us before. Jason, meet Alana Cooper. And what can I get you tonight?"

Jan placed a plate of warm garlic bread on the table for starters and by the time the main course arrived Alana knew that Jason was a surveyor working on a proposed subdivision on the edge of the village and he listened with interest about her graveyard project.

"The area I'm working on was originally part of the forest and there are a few old pieces of machinery lying around. There's even evidence of buildings on one area of the site which could create a few problems if they have any historic significance." Jason was well aware of the occasional conflict between commercial development and the desire to retain the past.

"I'd love to see the site if you don't mind showing it to me." For a moment Alana's enthusiasm made her forget her shyness. "That's if…" "I'd love to show you tomorrow if you want to meet me there. It's only a short drive along the side road near the river." It was almost nine o'clock by the time the meal was over and coffee was served in the small lounge.

After promising to catch up with Jason the next day, Alana returned to her room with a spring in her step. It had been a very pleasant evening and Jason was good company. Yes, she was really looking forward to meeting him again in the morning.

****

With the wedding ceremony behind them, Mary had discarded her hat soon after the photographs had been taken, letting her hair fall down around her shoulders. The day had been filled with excitement, starting with the wedding service itself taken by a visiting clergyman. The vows had been said and Florence had blushed when Walter took her in his arms and kissed her tenderly.

Then the guests were all invited to be part of the wedding portrait with the bridal party in the centre flanked by family members. Mary was aware of the presence of John Cameron during the ceremony and knew she would be seated beside him for the feast to follow. They had met at family occasions over the years, but today for the first time she realised what an attractive man he was with his smoothed back hairstyle and stylish moustache. "He'll think I'm just a silly child," she sighed as she adjusted her dress and smoothed the tiered skirt.

The festive lunch was set out on long tables under the shade of the fine oak trees and when the guests took their seats the meat was carved and the vegetables served. There was lamb, beef and turkey with potatoes and pumpkin and bowls of fresh peas and beans gathered that morning from the garden. Jugs of gravy and homemade chutneys and pickles completed the spread. Mary turned to John Cameron who had served her a succulent slice of lamb. She spooned some vegetables onto the plate and poured a little gravy on top.

"This is a most delicious meal and what a beautiful companion to be sharing it with." John smiled at the young lady at his side, one who had changed from a child to a handsome young woman almost before his eyes. Mary smiled back shyly and looked across the table to where her mother was sitting. She had already been admonished for removing her hat and now she was sure to be in more trouble if she appeared to be enjoying the conversation with John Cameron.

After the main meal a grand selection of sweet dishes appeared on the table. Fresh peaches from the garden, homemade ice cream, sponge cake and raspberries along with steaming pots of tea. Lighting up a cigar, John studied the young woman beside him. He had been so busy setting up his barber's shop and bath room that there was little time for socialising. His other great interest was fitness training and he encouraged the young athletes of the area to join his fitness school where they were taught the art of muscle building using a set of dumb bells.

Such was the success of his school that his pupils were performing in competitions and bringing a great deal of credit to his name. "A sound mind in a sound body" was his philosophy and he himself spent many hours in the exercise room perfecting his technique.

Turning back to Mary, John stroked the end of her long hair and complimented her on its beauty. "Come along to my bath house and I will see that your hair is plaited in the latest fashion," he offered. "I have just employed a young man who will create a special look for you."

Mary blushed and looked up at him with wide eyes. "I believe it costs four shillings for each plait. That would be well out of my price range as I have just finished my schooling and have not yet found employment." John smiled and said that the hair appointment would be a gift. "Besides, it would be a great advertisement for my saloon to have someone of your character come and pay me a visit."

It was true. The hairdressing saloon and bath room was mainly used by athletes, cyclists and football players who used the facilities as part of their training. At one shilling for a hot bath or six pence for a cold one, the establishment was especially busy after sports events and before the Saturday night dances in the town hall.

As the afternoon drew to a close it was time for dancing on the lawn beside the homestead. Seating had been arranged and a band struck up with the latest tunes. Walter and Florence were first on their feet for the traditional wedding waltz and then it was the turn of the bridal party to share in the dance. Mary found herself being swirled around in John's strong grip and her initial shyness soon gave way to the excitement of the occasion.

As the music came to an end, John held her for a moment longer than necessary, then led her back to the seats beside the rose gardens where a cool jug of ale was waiting on a wooden table. He silently filled two glasses of the amber liquid and handed one to Mary who accepted it with a twinge of guilt that she would be sharing an alcoholic beverage with a man she hardly knew.

But she noticed that most of the other family members and guests were also sampling the ale. She was surprised to see her father, Elias Gregg, with a large handle of beer and her mother holding a slim glass of the ale and taking small sips from time to time. After a few sips, the brew was still too bitter for her taste, so John thoughtfully added a little lemonade which helped to sweeten it.

"That is now a very pleasant drink. Especially after all that energetic dancing." "If you think that was energetic, wait until the polkas begin." John spoke in a teasing tone, allowing his arm to drape across her shoulder.

When it was time to leave, Elias gathered his family together and Mary reluctantly said goodbye to John Cameron. He held her hand for a moment and said: "I'm sure we will meet again, young Mary." Then she was helped up into the horse-drawn buggy and the happy group was soon on its way back to the Gregg family homestead.

Chapter 4

It was a cool crisp morning when Alana walked out to her car wearing a warm jacket over her jeans and carrying a cloth bag containing a writing pad, pen and her camera. If she was to see the old mill sites it could provide the chance to get some photographs to add to the historic records of the area.

As he had promised, Jason was waiting at the end of the side road which led into the dense pine forest. Alana locked her car and climbed into the four-wheel drive utility which Jason was using for his work. He had special permission to drive into the forest along the roads usually reserved for the workers and logging trucks, and as Alana buckled herself in she felt a ripple of excitement at the prospect of seeing the old mill remnants.

"I hope you don't mind a bumpy drive," smiled Jason. "I'll try to miss the worst of the pot holes but hang on just in case." Sure enough the next five minutes took them along a bumpy gravel road until Jason swerved into a clearing on the side of the trees. They were surrounded by young pine trees, probably about five years old with ferns and native plants struggling back through the fallen logs.

"We'll walk along the track from here to the site of the old sawmill." Jason was soon leading the way along the rugged track which was partially covered with bracken and fern. "It's a while since I came this way and the undergrowth is certainly starting to take over."

"How far is it to the mill site?" Alana asked as the track seemed to disappear into the new forest. "I'd hate to get lost in here. You'd never find your way out."

They trudged on in silence for about five minutes and Jason stopped to get his bearings. "We'll keep that steep rise to our left and follow the track a bit further. I'm sure we'll come across the clearing any time soon."

Sure enough, they came to a wide stretch of cleared land with piles of pine trimmings and a short gravel strip of road disappearing into the bush. They had reached the site of the former saw mill which had once employed many hundreds of workers. It took a few minutes to distinguish the remains of the concrete slabs and old metal machinery under the canopy of blackberry bushes and giant flax.

"It's hard to believe that so many workers were once employed here. Whatever happened to the logging industry?" Alana was curious. She could hardly picture the mill and the men who worked here. It was such a quiet, lonely place. Had John Cameron really been one of the workers here so long ago?

Jason produced a map from his knapsack and spread it out on the ground. The mill site is marked here," he said. "Many of the logs came down the river at this point and were lifted into the mill. The rest would have been hauled here by bullocks or horses."

They went closer to the stream where willow branches intertwined and soon came to a row of concrete pillars stretching up into the overgrown bush.

"We haven't much hope of going any further unless we bring some tools to cut back the bush. I'm not sure whether I want to be a lumberjack today." Jason smiled his warm smile and produced a chocolate bar. Alana accepted a few pieces of the rich dark chocolate before they turned towards the track that would take them back to the clearing where the utility was parked. She took out her camera and took a few shots of the stone pillars and rusty wheels and pipes.

"If I had a copy of the plan of the mill you would get a better idea of what it was like." As they headed back along the partially hidden track Jason kept his eye out for the remains of the workers' huts. The sight of a clump of apple trees was a clue and sure enough the old foundations of a building could be seen close to the track.

"There would have been a whole row of these huts along here. It would be interesting to unearth them one day and see if anything has been left behind. There's bound to be lots of old bottles and cans hidden under these ferns."

Alana was fascinated with the idea that so many people once lived in this small area. She would love to find the hut belonging to John Cameron and see if there was any clue left behind about the man and his life. There was probably an entry in the old rent book back at the museum to indicate which hut was John Cameron's or which boarding house he was living in.

But now Jason had work to do and Alana knew it was time to go back to Springvale and continue her work in the graveyard. As she unlocked her car Jason asked her to meet him for a drink and dinner later in the day.

Yes, she was most happy to do that and she drove off in happy anticipation of the evening ahead.

****

John Cameron's Hairdressing Saloon and Bath Room was set in the middle of the small township of Clifton, just south of the Scottish city of Dunedin, and on the main road leading to the very bottom of the South Island. The first settlement had been built high on the hillside but when the road was formed the businesses gradually relocated to the lower level. A thriving woollen mill was the chief employer in the town and pottery made from the high quality clay was finding its way into the homes of the nearby city.

Ornamental dishes and vases were not the only products being made at the pottery works but also baths, basins and toilet bowls which were finding a ready market in many of the finest homes being built in the area.

John had employed a young barber named Nick Postles, recently arrived from Glasgow and already proving popular with the young men of the town. He was keen to test his talents on the ladies too but few ventured into the establishment which was considered to be male territory.

"How do we entice the young women to come through our doors?" he asked John one morning. So far that day he had cut the hair of two business owners and one bachelor farmer. The mill workers usually arrived on a Saturday for a hair cut before heading to the local tavern or a barn dance on some farmer's property. Dances at the local hall were also well attended with the ladies sitting on seats around the dance floor while the men stood nervously just inside the door.

"Most women have their hair trimmed in their homes and learn how to twist it becomingly enough, but we could do a lot better, I know." John had been thinking about the problem for many months. "Perhaps we need to set up a special room with a feminine style of furnishings and offer tea and cake." The two men laughed at the prospect.

In the back room of the saloon, John was kept busy providing massage for strained muscles and stiff joints and he promoted a product called Every Athlete's Embrocation, which he said came highly recommended by a champion English athlete. He never really said who the athlete was, but the powerful smell and the heat from the potion seemed to work wonders and was widely used before and after training.

It would be good to build up the clientele and offer something for the women of the town. Not that they had the money for regular haircuts and they would probably be too shy to use the bath rooms, but there must be a call for a fancy hair arrangement on a special occasion. His thoughts returned to the wedding the previous weekend and he smiled at the memory of Mary's long shining hair. He had hardly recognized the young woman who was the niece of the bride. She and her family were often at the social functions and he had spoken to her father on the odd occasion.

He recalled that her grandfather had been the area's first school master, and her father farmed on a small holding a few miles from Clifton. Most of the sons had taken up farming although one was a saddler and another worked in the general store.

Her brother William had been one of the fitness school's first pupils and competed with success at the weight lifting competitions organized by the school.

Yes, it would be a great day indeed if he could persuade the likes of Mary and her sister to use the services of his saloon.

****

After leaving the old mill site, Alana decided she had better return to her work at the grave yard. She still had several rows of graves to photograph and record and then she would match them up with the cemetery records. She was intrigued by the remains of the workers' huts on the fringe of the forest. Was one of these once occupied by John Cameron all those years ago?

As she passed the lonely grave, she found an empty jar and filled it with water. Then she picked a few flowers from a wild rose bush and placed the jar at the end of the grassy mound. Did John Cameron have any descendants who might be wondering where he was buried?

Over the next two hours she continued her work and returned to the tavern and was greeted by the owners who were curious to know how her meeting with Jason had worked out. Jan Evans in particular was delighted that Alana had accompanied Jason to the mill site and hoped the friendship would flourish. There was nothing like a little romance to spice up her day.

Alana smiled as she headed up the staircase to her room on the top floor. She placed her bag on the chair and changed into a pair of sandals, then realised that she hadn't eaten lunch. She had the choice of going back to the café or making herself a sandwich in the kitchen of the tavern and bringing it back to her room. Choosing the latter, she made her way down the stairs and into the small cluttered kitchen behind the bar area.

She had the room to herself as the lunch rush was over. It didn't take long to butter some bread and choose the fillings from the fridge and she was back up the stairs to tackle the work of updating her computer records and downloading the latest photographs.

With just over two weeks to complete the work, Alana knew she would have to move faster and not spend so much time obsessing about the one grave which had stirred her imagination. Matching photographs and inscriptions to the names on the cemetery records was a simple process. But when there was an unmarked grave or some in a bad state of repair it was more difficult. In many cases, one or two names were engraved on the monumental stone but the official records often revealed others whose bodies or cremated remains were also buried there.

She would be glad to get back to Wellington after the job was finished and complete the paperwork. Then it would be time to find her next employer. Life as a museum graduate was proving to be full of uncertainties. Moving from one small town to another didn't leave much time for a social life, that was for sure.

She felt a tingle of anticipation at the thought of dinner with Jason tonight. He seemed like a really nice guy and the fact that he also lived in Wellington was a plus. But what was she going to wear? She opened the wardrobe in the corner of the room to search for something a little more exciting than her usual jeans and t-shirt. Right at the back there was a light silky blouse in pale grey. With a bright cerise camisole and her black cut-offs, that should be dressy enough for a dinner in the tavern. She was sure that Jason would be wearing casual attire. He was hardly likely to have brought anything upmarket while he was surveying the old mill site of Springvale.

It was almost five o'clock so Alana decided there was time for a shower and she would wash her hair. By the time she had dressed and applied a little make up her appearance was very different. She looked in the mirror and the image smiled back at her. Glossy dark hair with a hint of curl. Brown eyes highlighted with a touch of eye shadow. Skin slightly tanned from working in the outdoors.

She pulled on a pair of light sandals and made her way down the stairs to the dining room and bar. Bruce Evans looked up from where he was setting out glasses and gave a low wolf whistle. "You sure scrub up nicely, Alana. Got a hot date have you?"

Alana smiled and went in search of Jan. She wasn't sure what time Jason would be meeting her and she felt like chatting to the friendly woman. Jan was drinking a cup of coffee and was happy for Alana to join her. The evening rush would start soon although much of the work had already been done. Roast meat and vegetables were cooking in the large ovens and the salads had been prepared ready for the evening meals.

"We have a couple of bookings, but you never know how many will turn up for a meal," she laughed. "We have a few new items on the menu tonight so I hope you are dining in with us."

"As far as I know, I'm dining here with Jason but he could have ideas of going somewhere else. I think it would be hard to find anything to compare in this part of the country." Alana realized they had not confirmed where they would be eating but had assumed it would be the Springvale tavern.

At that moment, Jason put his head around the door. "I've just got back, so I'll go upstairs to tidy up. See you soon."

"I'm pleased that you are getting to know Jason. He seems like a very nice young man. I think his type of work can be a bit lonely at times with all the travelling involved." Alana felt a flash of sympathy. She knew exactly what it was like to be working away from home and being away from friends and family. Yes, she would understand Jason very well.

Chapter 5

"Come along Mary, there's work to be done." With a sigh Mary rose from the seat where she had been sitting, reading a newspaper which told of the social events of Dunedin and reports of cattle and horse sales. What fun it would be to live in the city where there was plenty of activity to fill the day.

Now she had left the high school where she had spent three years, what was there for her to do except help with the endless chores on the farm. Her father had high hopes of her becoming a teacher but the work was not to her liking.

"I wish I could go and live with my aunt and get a job in Dunedin. I'm sure I could find work in a store or maybe become a housemaid for a rich merchant," she sighed.

Her mother smiled at young Mary's restless ways. She was the eldest daughter with her sister Jean still at school and it was her role to help out in the house while her brothers tended the stock and worked on the land. The fields were now yielding rich pasture since the discovery of limestone on their property.

"The laundry bag is filled to overflowing and it's a great day for drying the clothing. Now fill the copper with water and set the fire beneath it. There's no time for day dreaming with so much to be done."

The large round copper was set outside the back door of the house under a rough shelter and Mary soon set about filling it with water which was pumped from the well. She then carried a bundle of dry firewood and placed it in the cavity under the copper. Soon the fire was lit and the water began to warm. There was soap to rub into the clothing before it was tossed into the water and then stirred around with a long wooden pole.

Mary's father Elias had recently purchased a mangle which was placed beside the copper and Mary had learned how to lift the linen and clothing from the copper and turn the handle to wring out most of the water. A tub of cold water had been placed beside the mangle and the clothing was rinsed to remove the soap before being put through the mangle for a second time.

Then it was time to hang the garments over the long wire which ran from the shed to a sturdy pole in the yard. Wooden clothes pegs held the washing in place and the warm breeze blowing in from the sea would have everything dry in no time.

Mary actually enjoyed the work and the feel of the freshly laundered linen which smelt faintly of lavender which had been added to the soap.

As she hung out the garments she had worn to her aunt's wedding the week before she thought about her handsome companion, John Cameron. She would dearly love to meet him again but knew her parents would consider him far too old for a young girl like herself. She would need to think of a reason to go into town and pass by his salon. It was much easier for her brother who spent many hours training at his fitness studio with the weights and dumb bells.

Yes, she would ask her father to drive her into town in the small cart. In fact, she could probably drive the pony herself or ride into town on horse back. With these thoughts running through her mind, Mary soon finished the arduous laundry chore in time to help her mother prepare lunch for the boys. William would soon be here with a small sledge and they would ride to the back of the farm where Elias and Thomas were ploughing the pastures ready for a winter crop.

It had taken many years for the land to be cleared and planted in pasture and now sheep grazed on the hills while cattle were reared on the lower slopes towards the road.

Mary wore a large hat to keep the sun from her face as they headed out across the bumpy paddocks. The men would boil some water over an open fire to make the tea, and the bread and cold pork with apple sauce and fruit cake to follow would be a welcome treat.

Young William was eager for the day's work to be over so he could ride into town to join the weightlifting class. He took every opportunity to show his developing muscles as he rolled up his shirt sleeves and raked some large stones left behind by the plough.

"So you think you'll attract a pretty girl with those muscles," his father laughed. "Soon you'll be a match for your teacher, Mr Cameron. Now, he's the one for showing off his muscles, that's for sure. Although he's loathe to put them to good use on the family farm."   It was well known that none of Donald Cameron's sons had taken up farming like their Scottish father, with one studying art in Melbourne, Australia, and another training as a banker in the city of Dunedin. "With just the two daughters at home, old Margaret could well do with some extra help on her acreage and that John is the one who should be doing the work."

Mary had heard stories about the Scottish family who arrived in the area the same time as her own Gregg ancestors. Although Donald was a humble ploughman, his mother was the daughter of a schoolmaster back on the

Scottish islands, and the family had been taught to read and write at an early age.

As each of the children performed well at school and won scholarships to study in Dunedin, Donald and his wife Margaret had continued to toil on the land, proud that their offspring had opportunities that they would never have had back on the small island in Scotland.

John Cameron had studied in Dunedin for a time and worked as a reporter on the city's largest newspaper, but his interest in fitness training and weightlifting had taken over and now he was trying to make a living from his salon and fitness school and living in a room above the shop.

"I notice that the handsome fellow had his eye on young Mary at the wedding." William loved to tease his sister who was always eager to meet his male friends. "Now, he'd be the one to tame her, don't you think?" They all laughed and Mary's face reddened.

Elias stepped in. "Don't talk about your sister like that William. She'll be married to a fine young man when the time comes."

Soon the food was eaten and the men returned to work. Mary and her mother decided to walk back to the house carrying the tin buckets which had held the food. It was a glorious day as the sun filtered through the oak trees which had been planted by the first settlers on the land from precious seed brought out from the old country. Yes, there were many reminders of their English homeland as the savage new country was tamed and made productive.

For Mary, whose grandparents had made the long journey across the sea, this was the only life she knew. This was the land of her birth and this was where she was happy to stay.

****

Jason smiled to himself as he climbed the stairs that led to the upper storey of the tavern. It had been a while since he had last asked a woman to dine with him. Alana seemed like an interesting person with a career similar to his own.

He had grown up in a small country town just outside Christchurch in the South Island and his university days at Canterbury were filled with socialising in the city centre and following the fortunes of the Crusaders rugby team. He had played in the lower grades but a niggling thigh injury had stopped him from advancing further.

He chose a clean shirt and trousers from the scant wardrobe and quickly showered and changed ready to join Alana. He had thought about driving to the next settlement for a meal but changed his mind when he saw that she was comfortably settled in the bar beside the dining room. Perhaps another time they could go further afield or maybe meet up in Wellington during the weekend if things went well tonight.

Alana had finished her coffee and was reading a magazine when he joined her a few minutes later. "How was your day?" They both spoke at once, then laughed and found stools by the bar where Jason chose a beer and Alana ordered a glass of wine.

"Well, my day was okay, except for trying to find boundary pegs that don't appear to exist. What about you?"

Alana recalled the day's events. "I'll have to hurry things along. There is another whole section of the graveyard to be photographed and entered into the computer. It's a fairly new area so the headstones are easier to read. It's always a surprise to find that there are other remains buried in the graves without their names on the stone." She laughed. "It must seem like a grim way to spend my day."

As they finished their drinks, Jan Evans came bustling by, carrying a basket of utensils. "There is a group coming in from a field day. It might pay to get to the dining room ahead of them if you are ready to eat," she warned. "Shall we go?" Jason asked and Alana followed him into the dining area where they found a table by the window. After consulting the wine list he chose a bottle of red and they took some time to study the menu which had been newly typed up that day. Lamb shanks and a chicken pot pie had been added to the options along with the roasts and salad choices.

"All this outdoor work makes me hungry so I'll go for the onion soup and then the lamb shanks," he said. Alana took longer to make up her mind. She was hovering between the chicken pie and the roast pork when Jan came over to take their order and she settled on the former.

Jan poured a sample of wine for Jason to try and then filled their glasses before returning to the kitchen. "She's sure a busy lady, doing all that work herself. I think Bruce lends a hand when needed as well as serving the drinks." Jason had stayed at the tavern often enough to learn the routine.

He was right because as he spoke, a group of 10 people were being seated at the long table at the other end of the room and Bruce was soon taking their drink orders. Jason waved to one of the young farmers whom he had met previously and the room was soon filled with loud voices and laughter.

"You can see that the dairy industry is in good shape," he said. "These guys are obviously enjoying the thought of a big pay out this season." It was all very familiar to Alana from her days on the family farm. There had been good years and bad during her childhood.

Soon the delicious food arrived and a second glass of wine was poured. More young people had arrived and glasses of beer were downed as they watched the rugby on the big screen on the wall. Plates of potato chips were passed around and the atmosphere became boisterous as they watched their teams battle for the trophy.

"So much for a quiet dinner." Alana pulled her chair closer to Jason so she could hear him above the noise. "How about an evening stroll after our meal?" Jason nodded in agreement so half an hour later they were walking through the town where the only store open was the take-away shop which sold fish and chips, toasted sandwiches and hamburgers and a western type diner at the end of the street.

The road led to a park with a pond where ducks were huddled together on the shore, heads tucked under their wings. A sluggish stream wandered off through the undergrowth towards the coast. "It's hard to imagine that this little stream once carried logs and produce to the port," said Jason. "Here I go again. I'm beginning to sound like my old history teacher."

Alana smiled. She had the same interest in her surroundings as Jason did. Always questioning and wondering about the stories from the past. "Don't worry. I'm the same way. I'm hoping to finish another history paper next year, and then apply for a permanent job at a museum somewhere around the country. Most are run by volunteers so vacancies are few and far between, but maybe I'll get lucky."

Jason thought about his own career. Surveying had seemed like a logical choice if you were interested in town development and liked the outdoor life. "I'll probably end up in some sort of planning department and hopefully set up in business at some stage."

By the time they returned to the tavern, the two were chatting away like old friends and sat at the bar for an Irish coffee. Most of the crowd had left but a few remained and the farmer who had recognised Jason earlier came over to join them. He introduced his girlfriend and before Alana knew it, another hour had passed and she was beginning to feel the effects of the long day.

Jason seemed in no hurry to end the evening, however, so she leaned over and gave him a light touch on the arm and headed for the stairway. There was plenty of time to catch up next day if that was what he wanted to do.

She felt a little confused as she climbed the stairs. Jason seemed like a really nice person and the evening had gone well. She would like to see him again tomorrow and wondered whether he felt the same way. Time will tell, she decided as she drifted off into a dreamless sleep.

Chapter 6

William Gregg could hardly wait for the day's work to finish so he could ride into town and meet his friends at the weightlifting class. Twelve of the older lads were practising for an exhibition that was to be held at the local school following the prize giving. William had attended the school until he left at age 14 to work on the family farm. Books and lessons were not for him, but he had taken a liking to the rigours of weight training under the guidance of John Cameron.

Several of the other weightlifters were already assembled when he arrived and he tied his horse to the rail outside the hall and went inside to change into training clothes and select the dumb bells which he would use. The School of Physical Culture promised its pupils an increase in health, strength and physical activity if they were to exercise with the dumb bells for an hour each day.

John Cameron was already warmed up and lifting 120 lb weights with one hand, muscles bulging under the strain. William would love to have the same physique and he was working hard at achieving it although he could not afford to attend the classes as often as he would like.

Following the warm up exercises, the class was ready to begin the routine that they had been rehearsing and the evening passed quickly. As William was returning his weights to the locker room, John Cameron approached him, smiling in a friendly manner. "You are doing very well, William. You will be one of my star pupils any time soon. Tell me, how is that beautiful sister of yours? It was a great pleasure partnering her at the wedding."

"She's okay, I guess." William did not take too much time to observe his sisters.

"Then give her my regards," said John and walked away to finish packing the gear into the cupboards.

It was a while since John Cameron had been so taken with a woman and his thoughts kept returning to Mary Gregg. She was young, that was true, but many a man sought a younger bride in these country towns. His restless nature had not left much time for courting but maybe now it was time to start thinking seriously about finding a companion and settling down.   Perhaps he should make a call at the Gregg homestead and get to know the family a little better. Living alone above his barber's shop was not ideal and if he returned to the family farm it would be right back into the type of life that he and his brothers had turned away from when they moved to town.

He felt guilty at times as his father had died a few years back while his mother was as hale and hearty as the day she had arrived from Ayrshire as a young bride. She and two of her daughters still lived on the farm which was currently leased by a wheat grower.

John had recently heard from his older brother James who was soon to return from Melbourne to take up a job with the tourist department, photographing health resorts and native activities. He had married while in Australia, and would also be reluctant to return to rural life.

The Gregg family had attended his father's funeral along with most of the residents of the district as old Donald had been held in high esteem in the neighbourhood. He was sure he would be welcome there. Yes, he would ride out to the property on Sunday afternoon and pay his respects.

****

By the time Alana dressed and arrived at the dining room for breakfast, there was no sign of Jason. She was disappointed as the evening before had ended when she left rather abruptly. Bruce Evans was setting up a table and immediately came over to take her order. "You just missed Jason," he said. "He had to leave early to head back to Wellington for an urgent meeting. He said to tell you he hopes to get back tonight in time for dinner."

Alana smiled. She had plenty of work to keep her busy today and having a friend to share dinner with was much better than eating alone.

The new sections of the cemetery were orderly and most of the graves well marked. She was soon on the job of photographing and making notes and it was lunch-time before she returned to the old section and Grave 24. The ancient graves were certainly more interesting and the unmarked plot still fascinated her. She would try to visit the museum again today and read more about the old mill site and the cabins where the workers had lived. There must be a plan of them somewhere and a record of who had lived there all those years ago.

Today she had brought along a sandwich and a drink and Jan Evans had included a piece of fruit cake in the pack. There would be time to visit the museum before she began her afternoon's work and luckily the curator Flo Avery was on duty. She smiled when she saw Alana and welcomed her into the cluttered building.

48

"I found another box of old photos and newspaper cuttings about the mill," she said. "You are welcome to have a look through them and see if there is anything of interest." Flo had also located a book which had been written about the timber mill several years earlier and Alana was soon absorbed in the story.

On the third page she came across a photo of the crude workers' huts built around a clearing with a group of mill workers standing around in heavy clothing and boots and caps. Most wore beards or moustaches and were smoking pipes. One of these could be John Cameron she thought, but it would be impossible to know which one.

The country was in a depressed state and unemployment was at a record high so the men would have come from over a wide area to take up the work on offer at the forest and timber mill, leaving their families behind.

As part of her research she was free to follow any stories of interest so the story of John Cameron could be part of her work. She read through the old newspapers and found articles on the workings of the timber mill and its impact on the local area. There were community events and dances with entertainment, and reading through many of these reports the name of John Cameron came up as "reciting some humourous verses from the old country".

It seemed that in the short time he lived at Springvale he had definitely made an impact. It was strange that no-one had remembered him on his death.

By the time she had finished downloading her photographs and transcribing her notes it was well past six o'clock and Alana decided it was time to go downstairs to think about dinner. There was no sign of Jason when she arrived and she felt a tinge of disappointment. Maybe she should eat out tonight at the only other eating place in town.

Just as she was about to leave, she caught sight of Jason coming in the front door of the tavern. He looked around and caught her eye and smiled. "Whew, I thought I might have missed you. Would you like to eat with me again tonight?"

"That would be great. I'll wait here until you are ready and we'll go and check out the rest of the town."

It wasn't long before they were on their way down the only street in town to the grill and pizza shop at the end of the road. Jason was full of the news of his meeting in Wellington and Alana filled him in with the highlights of her day. He took her hand as they walked through the deserted town and as they entered the restaurant they smiled at the checked table cloths and wild west décor. The only thing missing was the rodeo saddle on the pavement outside.

They ordered beer and wine and sat in a booth and listened to country and western music played from a juke box in the corner. "This sure takes me back a few years," Alana said. "I haven't seen a juke box forever." By the time the huge steaks and plates of fries and salad arrived they were ready to eat, almost imagining themselves in the outbacks of Texas.

Chapter 7

The town of Clifton was bustling as it was the day for the local stock sale which brought all the farmers into town. A few of their wives came along too, gathering at the tea shop to catch up on all the news of the district.

John Cameron stood in the doorway of his premises and surveyed the scene. He knew that Nick Postles would be busy soon as several of the single men would take the opportunity to visit the saloon for a shave and haircut; most of the married ones were taken care of by their wives back home.

It would be great if he could entice a few of the womenfolk into the saloon, but maybe the thought of the bath house behind the flimsy wall would frighten them away. It would take a lot of capital to make the premises suitable for female clients, but perhaps he could hire a woman to dress hair and apply creams and potions to the fair ladies' skins.

He sighed as he returned to his work which mostly consisted of massaging the muscles of athletes and football players who had over-worked on the sport field. His bottles of Every Athlete's Embrocation were earning him a meagre living, along with the income from the fitness school.

Luckily, as local correspondent for the city paper he sent in reports of sports events and news items which earned him a small fee for his efforts. For several months he had worked full time for the Dunedin paper, at the same time writing witty verses and short plays which were popular with the social set, but had left to follow his dream of setting up a fitness school.

51

But now he would write a short note to the Gregg family requesting a visit on Sunday afternoon. They would have returned home from their English church by then and be ready to receive visitors. His own family attended the Scottish church in the village, but John rarely found the time to go to either. He would tell the Greggs that he wanted to inform them of the progress of their son William at the weight lifting class. Maybe they could afford to pay for a few more lessons if they knew he was likely to become a champion.

Then he would take the opportunity to seek out their daughter and spend some time with her. That would be a most pleasant way to spend a Sunday afternoon. He must of course ask Nick to shape his hair and wax his moustache to make the right impression.

****

The week passed quickly for Alana with her work in the graveyard and further research at the Springvale museum. The history of the mill made interesting reading and gave her a good background of life in the area all those years ago. At one time Springvale was quite a large village with a wharf and small craft negotiating the narrow stream from the mill to the village, then on to the coast a few miles away.

Most evenings were spent in Jason's company and after their meal they often walked along the river bank or watched television in the tavern with the other young people who lived in the area and came in to socialise after working hours. It reminded her of the farming town where she had been raised and was a very different scene from her life in the busy city of Wellington.

As the week went on, Alana wondered whether Jason would suggest meeting in the city during the weekend. She would be travelling back to her flat on Friday afternoon and she wasn't sure what he had planned.

She was enjoying his company very much but it would be a big step to meet him in her other world away from Springvale. Seeing him in Wellington would put their friendship on a whole new level.

Then on the Thursday morning she received a text message from her cousin Nick who wanted a bed for the weekend as he planned to watch a rugby game at the stadium on Saturday night. He would sleep on the pull-out couch in the living room and no doubt want a meal at some stage. That was fine by Alana but would mean a visit to the supermarket when she got back to the city.

As it turned out, Jason left for Wellington on Thursday afternoon and no plans were made for a meeting in the city over the weekend. With plenty of work to do on her laptop, Alana decided to use the time to write her report and avoid the dining room crowd by eating a snack in her room. Part of the new section of the cemetery had now been photographed and all that remained was to check the burial register and finalise the list of names.

Friday morning dawned brightly and Alana was able to photograph the last two rows of head stones in perfect light. There was still time to gather information from the museum before driving back to Wellington. She was anxious to sort through the remaining boxes of papers and photographs.

"You are certainly taking this job seriously," Flo Avery commented. "I thought a young one like you would be off to the city as soon as you were able, not searching through old newspaper files and faded photographs."

Alana smiled. "You sound just like my mother," she said. "She can't understand my interest in old stuff either."

A battered photograph album took her eye and as Alana turned the pages she found photos of dances, weddings and other social functions. There were a number of scenes with actors playing various roles and she was fascinated with the gorgeous dresses and hats worn by the women. The men were equally elegant and several photographs featured a fine-looking man with a handsome curled moustache and dark wavy hair parted in the centre.

"This seems like a popular fellow. He appears in many of the pictures. It would be good to know who it is." She set the album aside and picked up a newspaper from 1910. There were the usual stories and articles and as she turned the pages she came across an advertisement that caught her eye. JS Cameron, hairdressing saloon and bath room.

"Oh my gosh! Come and look at this Flo. I've found the elusive John Cameron." Another advertisement advertised JS Cameron's School of Physical Culture with an outline drawing of a man with wavy hair, a moustache curled at the ends and bulging muscles. "And look here. I'm sure this is the same man as in the theatrical photographs. I really believe it is John Stirling Cameron himself."

Alana hurriedly photocopied the advertisements and photographs from the book and the similarity was amazing. So, as well as being a journalist and then a mill worker, it seemed that John Cameron had owned a hairdressing business and fitness school.

"What paper are you reading?" Flo asked. "It doesn't look like a local one to me. Look at that. It's from the South Island, a little place called Clifton. That's miles away from here. The poor man certainly died a long way from home."

Alana knew that the newspapers from Clifton could give many valuable clues about John Cameron. She would search the old copies on the computer when she got back to Wellington. In fact, she may as well head back now. There was no reason to stay any longer in Springvale and with Nick coming for the weekend, there was plenty to keep her busy back at her flat in the city.

She chose the coast road back to Wellington, enjoying the sight of the breakers along the shore. As she got closer to the city, the old beach suburbs had now merged into one, with palatial homes taking over from the week-end baches which had once lined the shore.

An hour later she pulled up outside her apartment and parked her car in the garage behind the building. She climbed up the steps and unlocked the door. The room smelt musty, so she pulled back the curtains and opened a window to let in the breeze.

She tossed her bag into the small bedroom then opened the refrigerator to inspect the contents. After living in the tavern it was going to be difficult to remember to buy enough food and cook for herself. A trip to the super-market was going to be necessary before she did any-thing else.

Chapter 8

Saturday turned out to be a typical blustery Wellington day with a strong wind blowing in from Cook Strait and cloudy skies. Having set up the pull-out bed in the corner of the living room ready for Nick's arrival, Alana settled down at her desk with her computer and began checking the newspapers from Otago in the hope of finding more on the life of John Cameron. She already had a file of documents which she had collected from the museum in Springvale.

The local paper for Clifton came up with several references for John Cameron, many of them advertisements for his salon and weight-lifting school. There were also descriptions of social functions in the district describing his songs and poems which were always well received. One advertisement stated that he had sold the bath house and salon to Nick Postles but he was still advertising his weight-training classes.

There was no record of a marriage for John, but she found one for a William Cameron whose wedding was held in Clifton, followed by a dance in the barn at the bridegroom's father's farm. Could this be a brother for John Cameron?

Alana was so absorbed with the story which was developing that she lost track of time and was startled to hear a bang on the door downstairs heralding the arrival of her cousin Nick. "Hi, anyone home?" Before she knew it he had bounded up the steps and seemed to fill the small apartment as he threw his duffle bag down on the makeshift bed and stood by the window to take in the view of the waterfront down below.

"Great day for a game of rugby. How about joining me?" But Alana shook her head, and agreed to meet him after the match in a small bar down on the harbour. Left to herself again she decided to put on a jacket and take a stroll along the breezy waterfront. Too much time spent on the computer needed to be compensated with a brisk walk once in a while.

First she passed the high rise buildings which had replaced the earlier houses, then crossed the street to follow the sea wall all around the waterfront. A large cargo ship was being escorted into the harbour and several small yachts were competing out in the bay. Soon she reached the sandy beach at Oriental Bay where children played on the sand as they had done for generations. The old band rotunda and changing sheds which now housed a restaurant was still a focal point of the bay.

She paused to look at the houses on the hill, admiring the old kauri villas with their Victorian facades and elegant trim. One of the smaller properties was being demolished and she knew another apartment building would soon replace it, lodged against the rock cliff face, but the stately homes on the hillside would remain as part of the city's heritage.

She shivered in the breeze and retraced her steps, stopping for a coffee which she sipped as she walked back along the wide pavement that served as footpath and cycle track. Skateboarders and small children on cycles, mums and dads with infants in buggies and couples walking or jogging were all part of the busy scene.

Before she knew it, it was time to catch up with her cousin at the old boat house which had become a popular meeting place. It was a short walk from her apartment and she arrived before he did, found a table inside and ordered a glass of wine. A large-screen television was playing the highlights of the big game which had just been won by the local team, so she knew the boat house would soon be crowded with enthusiastic rugby fans.

Soon she saw Nick's large frame appear at the door, his fair hair tousled and a warm scarf wrapped around his neck. He ordered a beer from the bar and joined her at the table.

"You missed a great game. A bit too close for comfort but the boys did well to hang on." She laughed at his enthusiasm. Seeing grown men having their faces pushed into the mud wasn't her cup of tea, but she admitted to watching a game if the national team, the All Blacks was playing. She told him a little about her work in Springvale and caught up with his life back on the farm at Taupo. Yes, his parents were well and sent their regards.

Nick had recently completed an engineering course at the local polytech and was looking for work somewhere in the area. "But I'd really like to go to Australia and find work there. That's where all the action is these days," he admitted.

Alana shared her fears at not being able to find a steady job to match her career, but they laughed and agreed that they were too young to take it all too seriously at this stage.

The boat shed was soon crowded so they decided they would be better off to make a meal back at the apartment. Just as they were leaving, Alana thought she recognised Jason at the back of the crowd. Nick had gone on ahead so she hastened to join him, thinking it was probably her imagination and soon they were head-

58

ing up the steps and into the warmth of the cosy flat. No, she would forget Jason while she was back in Wellington.

In the meantime, Jason was enjoying a cool beer as he joined the after-match crowd at the boat house. He looked up at one stage and caught a glimpse of Alana leaving the building. He was about to attract her attention when he noticed her companion. He had been thinking about inviting Alana out to dinner while they were back in Wellington and now it looked as though she had a boyfriend already.

Even though they hardly knew each other he felt a stab of disappointment. He would like to be sharing time with her now but it was obviously not to be.

****

John Cameron had received a favourable response to his letter to the Gregg family and set off on his horse on Sunday afternoon to visit the farm which was set in a sheltered valley upon which lime deposits had been found. The spreading of lime had proved so beneficial to pasture growth that Mary's father was now selling it by the ton to supplement the income from the farm.

Elias' parents had taken up their allotted property back in 1864 when colonisation was at its peak and as well as being the area's first school teacher, he had farmed the land for many years, raising a family and taking part in many of the activities in the area. However, as most of the local settlers were from Scotland, they did not share in the church activities with the Presbyterians, but worshipped instead at the small Anglican church on the outskirts of Clifton.

The family had gathered in the front room which was only used on special occasions. The curtains were usually drawn to keep the sun off the furniture which had been brought out from England more than 40 years before. The over-stuffed sofa and high-backed chairs, heavy wooden dresser and china cabinet filled with favourite ornaments and memories of the 'old country' created a formal atmosphere. A large framed photograph of Elias and Mary on their wedding day dominated the wall above the fireplace.

Mary Gregg had baked a delicious chocolate cake and a variety of crisp biscuits which young Mary and her sister helped to serve. Balancing the delicate china cups on their flimsy saucers, the young women looked shyly at their guest as he spoke to Elias about the future of his son William.

"Your lad is showing superior skills as a weight lifter and will be the star of the show when we perform at the school next month," John was saying. "I would like to offer him special tuition if he can find the time away from the farm."

Elias looked a little doubtful but William's mother was impressed that her son could be a champion. "I'm sure that could be arranged. Don't you think so Elias?" She smiled at her husband. "Now, would you like to hear our daughter play for you on the pianoforte. I think you will agree she also has talent, but of a different nature."

John was delighted to sit and listen as young Mary played a selection of classical tunes with great finesse. When she had finished he applauded spontaneously and she blushed becomingly as she looked in his direction.

"Mary, my dear, perhaps you could show our guest around the garden and then we will all join you for a glass of sherry in the gazebo." Elias was proud of his overgrown garden which was planted in a wide variety of English flowering plants and shrubs. Brick paths bordered by low hedges separated the garden beds and a covered archway led to the gazebo at the edge of a smooth green lawn.

John followed Mary along the narrow path, admiring the blooms as they went. He was also admiring the young woman, with her shapely figure and long silky hair tied back in a loose knot. She wore a large straw hat to keep the sun off her face but as soon as they reached the gazebo, she took off her hat and laid it on the seat.

"I did enjoy your performance, my dear. I hope to hear you play at the end of year social at the school. You could accompany me when I give a rendition of some old Scottish ballads, I'm sure."

"I don't think I'm good enough for that, sir." Mary stammered. "I haven't performed in public and there are many other accomplished musicians in the area."

John knew that this was true. There was no shortage of musical talent in the Clifton area and the local Glee Club gave them the chance to show off their skills as they performed short plays and musical items.

"Do you have a career in mind? I'm sure a bright young lady like you could become a teacher like your grandfather."

"I'd really like to live with my aunt in the city and find work in a fashionable store," Mary said. "But I doubt that my parents would allow it. I am much too useful here on the farm."

John smiled. "All parents are the same in that way. I remember the fuss when my brothers and I gave up the farming life to study in the city. But they get over it and I feel that you must do what your heart tells you to do."

"You studied at the university for a time didn't you? I hear you completed a course in journalism before you came back to Clifton to open up your business. I would have thought that working for a large city newspaper would have been very interesting." Mary was curious about John's past.

"Most of my time was spent describing the gowns that fashionable women wore to social events. You have no idea the trouble one can get into by writing that a dress was made of satin when in fact it was pure silk or omitting an important person from the list."

Mary laughed as she remembered the recent account of her aunt's wedding in the local paper. Her dress had been described as maroon when she considered it to be scarlet and the fact that the bride's veil had belonged to her grandmother in Ireland had been left out altogether.

But now their conversation was interrupted as William came along the path carrying a silver tray with a decanter of sherry and several small crystal glasses which he set down on a round table in the corner of the gazebo. Mary's parents followed closely on his heels and soon Elias was filling the glasses with the amber liquid and passing them around.

"So what does a Scotsman think of my traditional English garden?" he asked.

"As I have never set foot in either England or Scotland it is hard for me to comment, but English or not, it is certainly a very fine garden and a credit to your endeavours. I myself have no time for a garden, living as I do above the bath saloon."

62

"I believe your mother still keeps a vegetable garden, even though the farm is now leased out for wheat growing." Mary's mother was curious about Margaret Cameron who had come to the area as a young bride. "I believe your younger sisters are the only ones still living with her on the farm."

"That's true. None of my brothers wanted to remain on the land, though we spent many hours helping to clear the scrub so my father could plough the land when we were very young."

"Your father was known as a talented ploughman. His skills are still talked about when country folk get together." Elias poured another glass of sherry as he recalled the old days in the district when the now fertile pastures were covered with bush and fern. A house site would have to be cleared before the women and children moved there from the barracks in Dunedin city.

By now the young people had become bored with the conversation and they suggested a game of croquet using the mallets and hoops from a box in the corner of the gazebo. It wasn't long before two teams were formed and John Cameron found himself partnering young Mary while William and his sister Jean made up the second team and the afternoon ended on a very pleasant note.

Chapter 9

As Alana drove the few kilometres back to Springvale after a busy weekend in Wellington, she was suddenly conscious of the fact that her work at the graveyard would need to be completed by the end of the week. She could then complete her assignment in her own time back in Wellington.

The day was warm and sunny so she dropped her bag at the tavern and walked the short distance to the graveyard with her camera slung over her shoulder. The grass had recently been mown and fresh flowers had been placed on a number of the more recent graves.

The older section of the cemetery was deserted, the weathered headstones shadowed by the tall trees which grew along the fence line. A small patch of yellow dandelions sat undisturbed on the grassy plot which covered the remains of John Stirling Cameron.

Alana could picture the man who had become so familiar to her. His muscular build, the dark wavy hair, handsome moustache and sparkling eyes. If she half closed her eyes, the image was almost real.

But there was no time for day dreaming. The last section of the newest area of the graveyard needed to be photographed to complete the project. She also wanted to find the time to return to the museum to continue her search of the photographs and records that the archivist had made available.

With any luck, Flo Avery might be at the museum around lunch time so just before noon, Alana bought herself a sandwich and drink from the café and made her way to the museum where Flo was just finishing up after a morning's work.

"Hullo Alana. I found some more papers and articles you might be interested in," she said. "You are most welcome to sit in my office and search through them while I go off for lunch." And with that, Flo bustled off leaving Alana alone in the crowded room with filing cabinets and shelves full of books and papers.

Alana smiled. Only in a small village like Springvale would you trust a stranger so quickly and give someone access to the treasures of the town. For the next hour she was kept absorbed as she ate her lunch and read through the stack of documents and newspapers on the cluttered table.

There were many accounts of the workings of the timber mill and the opening of the brewery which used water from a spring in the town to make its famous beer. No doubt John Cameron would have enjoyed a pint or more after a hard day's work at the mill.

Alana looked once more through the photographs to see whether she had missed one of John Cameron the last time she was here. She was certain that the sketch of John with the moustache curled at the ends was the man in the theatrical photos. The fact that the old newspaper from a town so far away was here in the Springvale Museum was certainly a coincidence.

****

Following his pleasant afternoon at the Greggs' homestead, John Cameron was keen to meet again with their attractive daughter. He was bewitched with the young woman and felt that she might have feelings for him as well. The difference in their ages didn't trouble him as many men in their 30s chose younger brides when the time came to marry.

The opportunity to meet her again came up the next week when he was asked to entertain at a social gathering to be held in the local hall. He and his friends from the Glee Club were to perform a short play which they had been rehearsing and he would sing one of his humorous Scottish ballads. This would be followed by supper and dancing.

Without wasting any time, he wrote an invitation to the Gregg family hoping that the older Greggs would bring the young daughters along. His light-hearted mood was noticed by the young barber. Nick Postles was also eager to meet a young woman as he knew few people in the town, so John told him about the social evening and invited him along.

As they shared a pint of ale after closing time, the two men reflected on the chances of meeting any suitable marriage partners in such a small town where the women were closely guarded by their families.

"It's no wonder the town is full of bachelors like myself," sighed John and his friend agreed. There was certainly a shortage of available females in the town of Clifton.

****

With her satchel full of notes and camera loaded with grave photographs Alana spent the rest of the afternoon in her room at the Springvale tavern. She matched the photographs of the headstones and bare areas of grass with the list of numbered burial plots, building up a picture of the town as it changed through the years. Family groups were popular with many generations now lying side by side and a few lonely graves with barely any detail on the notes or inscriptions. Many of these were possibly mill workers who had been attracted by the money on offer during the depression years.

Men like John Cameron who had left his South Island home and business to seek work at the mill.

She was so absorbed in her task that she hardly gave a thought to Jason, who had not yet returned from Wellington. She would like to have met him over the weekend but the arrival of her cousin Nick had intervened. She wondered again whether she had seen Jason in the crowd at the old boat house. It would have been great to have met him there.

Maybe he was back by now and they could have a meal together and catch up on their news. Taking a moment to comb her hair and freshen up her make up, Alana almost ran down the staircase and into the foyer below. Through the doorway she could see Bruce Evans setting up the bar for the evening. Monday was usually a quiet night for the local trade.

Jan Evans was already in the kitchen and greeted Alana with a smile. "Well, how was your weekend in the big smoke? I guess you had a great time catching up with friends."

"It was okay. My cousin from Taupo stayed over and we braved the rugby crowd down by the waterfront. I thought I saw Jason there but I wasn't sure. There were so many people."

"He phoned to say he wouldn't be back tonight, but he should be here in the morning. Would you like to eat dinner down here or in your room tonight?" Alana felt a twinge of disappointment at having to dine alone, but thought she might just as well eat dinner in her room where she could read a book or watch the news on television.

"One of your yummy steak pies would be good, and whatever else you have to offer," she said and went back to her room which now seemed rather bleak and lonely. She turned on the television and let it play in the background as she sorted her notes from the museum.

An hour later, Jan knocked on the door with a tray full of food and a small bottle of wine. The pie smelled delicious along with creamy mashed potato and fresh green beans. She opened the bottle of wine and poured some into the glass tumbler and took a sip. There was a generous slice of apple crumble with a dab of cream to follow.

It sure had been nice having someone to share a meal with every night and she was beginning to get used to the company. But in a few days' time she would be back to her old life in Wellington until the next assignment took her to another town. She only had the rest of the week to get to know Jason better so she would make the most of their time together.

Chapter 10

As Jason drove along the busy highway towards the small village of Springvale he thought about his schedule for the week ahead. His work on the mill site should be completed over the next two weeks and his next assignment had not yet been decided.

Having no family close by, his job as a surveyor suited him for the moment as he was free to travel at short notice. His small apartment in the Hutt Valley was ideal and just a short train ride into the city at the weekends where he could take in a game of rugby and catch up with a few mates for a beer.

It didn't give him much time for a steady girl friend but there was plenty of time for that. He had fully intended to ask Alana to meet him in the city but missed the opportunity when he returned to Wellington earlier than expected.

Seeing her with that guy at the old boat shed had taken him by surprise. She had never mentioned having a boy friend but it looked as though he was out of luck there. Maybe he should send her a text message and ask her to have dinner with him. No, it was probably better to play it cool for the rest of the week and not get his hopes up in that direction.

His mind was full of indecision as he drove into the car park of the country tavern and took his bag from the back of the wagon. Alana's car was parked closer to the building but she usually walked the short distance to the cemetery or museum.

Jan Evans came out of her office as he walked through the front entrance. She gave him a warm smile and asked how his weekend had gone. "You have just missed Alana. She was headed for the cemetery last time I saw her. By the way, she said she might have caught a glimpse of you down by the waterfront after the rugby but she wasn't sure. Too many people. That's what she said."

"I thought I saw her at the back of the crowd at one stage, but I could have been mistaken," was Jason's reply. "We will probably catch up for a drink together when we get back tonight. In the mean time I had better get changed and be on my way."

Jan watched with amusement as he went up the stairs. "There could be a budding romance going on here," she said to Bruce as he came out from the kitchen. "I haven't seen Jason so interested in a young woman before."

"You're a born romantic, Jan my love. But between you and me, they'll probably just be like two ships passing in the night."

****

With the social evening coming up in a week's time, John Cameron and the rest of members of the Glee Club began polishing up their items for the big event. He had sent an invitation to the Gregg family asking them to be his guests and he promised them good seating at the best table. He knew they were regular attendees at the Church of England on the hill and hoped that the nature of some of the skits and songs would not offend them in any way.

He had to make sure his own performance was not too bawdy on this occasion and chose a humorous recitation and two songs from the Scottish highlands which always proved popular. Several of the women who lived in the town were busy preparing a number of tasty dishes for the supper and there would be a plentiful supply of beer and spirits to please the men folk.

Two days before the function he received a note from Elias Gregg confirming that he and his wife would be accompanied by their two elder daughters and would be happy to accept John's gracious invitation. On receiving the letter, John rubbed his hands together as he entered the barber's shop to find Nick Postles. "Nick, my lad. Make sure you spruce yourself up. There are at least two attractive young ladies coming to the social. Keep your eyes off young Mary but I will be pleased to introduce you to her sister. It promises to be a very fine occasion indeed."

Back at the Gregg homestead, Mary and Jean were excited at the prospect of an evening out in Clifton. They looked through their dresses and decided they had nothing suitable to wear but their mother trimmed their best gowns with a few decorative touches and knew they would suit the girls well.

She was proud of her daughters who had grown into attractive young women in such a short time. "It only seems the other day that they were small children and now look at the pair of them," she confided in her husband. Elias smiled in her direction. "And young men will be courting them. Of that I am sure. I think that John Cameron already has designs on young Mary, but he is surely twice her age."

"We will keep an eye on her, but she is at a fashionable age to start courting," Mary sighed. "And he does appear to be a perfect gentleman."

The weather remained fine for the evening of the Glee Club social with just a light breeze and no hint of showers. The Gregg family climbed into the dray which was pulled by two horses. The wooden seats around the sides were piled with cushions and there were warm rugs to cover their legs if they were needed.

As they approached the hall in the middle of town, Elias turned the horses into a side paddock and hitched them to a rail. There they would stay for the evening munching on the oats and hay from a wooden tray in front of them. The building was well lit with lanterns, and a piano was being played with gusto as they went inside.

John Cameron looked splendid in a bowler hat and stiff-collared shirt. He guided them towards a table with a good view of the stage, making sure that there was space for him to sit beside young Mary who blushed prettily at the attention.

It wasn't long before drinks were being offered along with plates of bread, cheese and pickled onions. "This is just to get us started," said John. "The main course will follow after the first items."

Once the crowd was seated two young women made their way to the piano and set up a sheet of music on the stand. They played two Chopin melodies with flair, then stood and bowed and returned to their seats. "You could do as well as that," John whispered to Mary, who giggled shyly. "But now it's my turn."

The crowd applauded as John Cameron made his way to the small stage at the front of the hall. He wore his bowler hat at a jaunty angle and carried a small cane for added effect as he launched into the humorous tale of a ring-tailed raccoon. He had performed the piece many times and was greeted with even more applause as he finished the item and returned to his seat.

"A great story! Most enjoyable evening." Elias Gregg was warm in his praise and shook John by the hand. "You are very welcome to come to our home any time and entertain us." By then the meal was ready and everybody lined up to pile food onto plates. There were several choices of meat with an array of fresh vegetables and rich brown gravy.

The townsfolk filled their plates and congratulated the women on the fine spread, before returning to their tables where the noise and laughter was more subdued as they enjoyed the meal. Several returned to refill their plates while others waited for the desserts to be served.

Mary ate slowly, glancing up at John from time to time. She was pleased to be with him but didn't know what to say or how to act. He frequently looked in her direction, taking in the fine features, shy smile and mid-brown hair which had been piled up in a becoming manner.

He looked across at the next table where young Nick Postles was sitting with a friend from the fitness school and remembered his promise to introduce him to Jean Gregg when the opportunity arose. "I'm sure my friend Nick would like to meet your sister if it can be arranged," he said. "He is a fine young fellow who runs the barber's shop in my bath house. Having recently arrived from the old country he hardly knows anyone in the town."

Mary looked over to where Nick sat with the other young lads. He looked like a pleasant young man and was certainly better groomed than most. She turned to Jean who sat beside her and pointed him out. "John wants you to meet his young friend Nick. We could have some fun when the dancing starts."

They knew there would be a few more musical items after the meal and then the tables would be taken away and the floor cleared for dancing. Mary was looking forward to the chance to dance once more with John who had proved to be such a good partner at the wedding. Jean nodded in agreement and the two young women grew impatient for the items to be over and the dancing to begin.

Chapter 11

When it was time for Flo Avery to close the museum, Alana had gathered a great deal of information about the timber mill and the people who lived in Springvale during the town's heyday. Although the rest of the country was feeling the effects of the Depression, the income from the timber was keeping the town more buoyant than most.

Many hundreds of workers had been attracted to work in the forest or the mill and several boarding houses as well as three hotels catered for the men who had come from all parts of the country. In the beginning, a number had camped out in a tent city alongside the river in very primitive conditions or in the simple huts close to the mill.

Remembering the details on John Cameron's burial record, Alana thought it more likely that he had been living in a boarding house and she wondered how it would be possible to find out. When she returned to Wellington she would look up the Census figures for around the time. They usually listed the names of the people in each dwelling house but only if they were there on Census night.

Arriving back at the Springvale tavern she looked around for Jason's vehicle but he had obviously not returned. It would be good to meet him for a drink before dinner and maybe share a companionable meal as they had done over the past weeks. With this in mind she took a little extra time to wash and dress before going downstairs to check out the night's menu.

As she crossed the foyer to get to the bar and dining room, Jason was just coming through the door. He looked dusty and tired from his day out in the forest clearing but his face lit up when he saw her. "Hi Alana. Good to see you. Give me time to shower and change and we'll catch up soon."

There was a new spring in his step as he climbed the stairs and Alana watched him go with a feeling of excitement as she realised that she had missed him over the past few days. Jan Evans came out of the office at that moment and welcomed Alana, insisting that she share a coffee with her. "It's the only break I'm likely to have all evening as the farmers' group will be back for dinner and we have a few extra guests staying tonight."

Alana was constantly amazed at Jan's energy and the way there was always enough food no matter how many guests came in for dinner. She would miss this companionship when she returned to Wellington next week. She had been content in her small apartment on the side of a hill in the bustling city, but there she rarely spoke to anyone. It seemed that small town living was much more friendly.

It didn't take Jason long to tidy up and return to the dining room where he came over to Alana and gave her a friendly squeeze. "I'm beginning to feel really spoilt staying here. I'll miss all this company when I get back to my place in the Hutt." Alana couldn't believe that he was voicing her feelings.

"I was thinking exactly the same thing. This place is so special. I think I will always remember it. Maybe we should find a quiet table in the corner as the farmers are meeting here soon and you know what that's like."

Alana led the way to a small table in a booth as far away from the bar as possible. Bruce looked over in their direction and poured them their usual drinks. A white wine for Alana and a beer for Jason were soon delivered to their table. "I recommend the chicken pot pie tonight. It's one of Jan's specialties."

"We won't be ready for a while. There's a bit of catching up to do," said Jason, as he picked up his glass and twirled it around, admiring the golden glow of the locally brewed beer. "Here's to your last week in Springvale. I hope your assignment will be a success."

Alana raised her glass to his and smiled into his eyes. "It's been great. Much better than I thought it would turn out, but there is a lot more I want to learn about my favourite character, John Stirling Cameron."

Jason was about to ask Alana about her weekend when the first of the young farmers' group came into the bar. They waved in Jason's direction then settled themselves on the bar stools as Bruce poured tall glasses of the frothy brew straight from the tap.

"I thought I saw you at the old boat house," they both spoke at once, then laughed.

"Yes, I was there after the rugby match and I'm sure I saw you as you were leaving," Jason was anxious to hear Alana's reply.

"I called in after the match to catch up with a friend but it was too crowded so we left and went back to my flat." Alana wasn't sure why she called Nick her friend and not her cousin and Jason's face clouded over.

"It sounds as though you had a good time. I guess you have many good friends in Wellington. You have lived there longer than I have." Jason picked up their empty glasses and took them over to the bar. It was a while before he returned with another drink and Bruce followed him over to the table to take their orders.

With the dining room now full and the noise level rising, Alana and Jason sat in silence for several moments. Alana had the feeling that something was upsetting Jason and she didn't want anything to spoil the rest of their time together.

"Actually, apart from my friend Angela, I don't really know anyone in Wellington. I guess my job makes me a bit of a gipsy like yourself. And by the way, the friend I met at the boat shed was my cousin Nick, up for the weekend from Taupo."

"Well, in that case I hope you will count me as a friend, especially when we get back to Wellington." Jason was smiling now just as Bruce appeared with two portions of chicken pot pic and a plate of vegetables.

"Enjoy your meal, my friends," he said, as he put the plates down with a flourish. He winked at Jason. "And the best of luck to the pair of you."

Chapter 12

After a great evening of entertainment, followed by dancing, the Gregg family returned to their farm in good spirits. Mary and Jean huddled into the blankets as the cart swayed as it bounced along the country road.

"How did you get on with Nick?" Mary was curious to know. Her sister had joined in a number of energetic dances with the young barber.

"He is a nice enough lad. But what about yourself? I saw you dancing very close to a certain Mr John Cameron." Jean laughed as she teased her older sister. "Is he going to ask you to walk out with him?"

Mary glanced towards her parents who were sitting on the front of the dray. Elias was expertly driving the two horses and concentrating on avoiding the worst of the pot holes. "I'm not sure. He probably thinks I'm just a child, but he does seem to be showing an interest in me." Mary knew she was beginning to have feelings for the handsome man but apart from living with her brothers and sharing a classroom with a number of unruly males, she had little experience of the opposite sex. John Cameron was handsome and charming but she felt shy in his presence.

She would like them to become better acquainted but it was difficult when she lived so far out in the country. Although she had been happy to leave the classroom behind her, these days Mary felt discontented with her life and often asked if she could live with her aunt in the city and work in her store where they sold drapery and haberdashery.

She would meet any number of fancy fellows in Dunedin, a city known for its busy social scene. Imagine wearing a different dress each day and handling all that beautiful cloth and choosing the trimmings for a perfect gown. It would be a far cry from life on the farm where helping with the laundry and cooking scones and cakes over a hot stove took up most of her day.

Young Jean was still going to the local school, which Mary had also attended. Jean had no desire to work on the farm but had ambitions to become a school teacher. She was already working as a pupil teacher, helping with the younger children in the crowded classroom until she gained her teaching certificate.

"I wish our parents lived in Dunedin where life would be much more pleasant," Mary confided to her sister. "I think our father should sell the farm to the man who owns the lime works company. I know they are anxious to mine the lime deposits on our land."

Since the discovery of the benefits of spreading lime on the fields, the rich deposits in parts of the district were highly sought after. The limestone was also used for roads and drive ways and Elias was now making more money from selling lime than from milking their few cows and raising sheep.

The air was cool as they travelled along the bumpy country road towards the farm. Mary pulled the rug more closely around her. Would John Cameron want to see her again? She felt a shiver of excitement at the idea of walking out with him. She would ask her parents to invite him to afternoon tea and she could accompany him on the piano as he sung his favourite Scottish tunes.

****

As John Cameron returned to his rooms above the salon, he was thinking of Mary and wondering how he could get to know her better. His new partner, Nick Postles, was anxious to offer hairdressing for women and had already had a sign printed for the window which offered a range of services for both men and women. "Ladies hair cutting and singeing a specialty, all descriptions of work done. Plaits from 4 shillings each." With Nick so keen on the hairdressing side of things, John could see the time when he would be able to concentrate solely on the fitness school and sales of his embrocation. A number of his pupils were preparing for the competitions which would be held in December, along with a public exhibition, and training days and nights were keeping him busy.

However, the business was not lucrative and he had little to offer a prospective bride, unless he returned to his journalism career in the city. He was anticipating a small share when his mother eventually sold the family farm.

With James at art college and William working in a Dunedin bank, his twin sisters helped out on the farm. John often wondered how his parents, who came to New Zealand as a ploughman and dairy maid, had managed to raise such an intellectual family.

Monday was a quiet day in the town of Clifton and Nick spent some time rearranging the salon, still working on the idea of enticing a few ladies to use their services. He would love to invite Jean, his young dancing partner from the previous weekend, to try out the new facilities. It was amazing what a coat of whitewash and new covering for the shabby chairs had done. With the addition of a wash basin and large mirror on the wall, the ladies' section of the salon was almost ready for customers.

Even in the small town of Clifton, women were beginning to display their independence, although the feminist movement was strongest in the cities.

"What do you think about inviting Mary and Jean to be our first customers? I would give them a free hair cut, and shampoo and style their hair in any fashion they chose," he said. "It would be a good advertisement for the new ladies' salon."

"I hope all the fancy additions won't deter our male customers," John laughed. "But on the other hand they might be keen to check out the talent. I have already broached the subject with Mary but now I will send a note to the young ladies and await their reply with interest."

The arrival of the newspaper from Dunedin interrupted the conversation and as John read the headlines, noting that two of his stories had been published, he let out a shout. "I see that our Prime Minister King Dick is to pay a visit to Clifton next week. The whole town will turn out to welcome him." Richard Seddon was a popular Prime Minister who had done much to bring about social reform to the young nation and was sure to attract a crowd.

"I'm sure the Gregg family will be in town for the occasion. We will have to make the most of the opportunity to see the young ladies again." John put down the newspaper and returned to the massage room at the rear of the salon, his thoughts on the young woman who had caught his attention.

****

After a very good dinner and a bottle of wine, Alana and Jason were not ready for the evening to finish so after getting jackets from their rooms, they set out along the deserted street towards the park and the river bank. There was enough moonlight to show the way and Alana felt quite light headed as she held Jason's hand and walked in silence beside him.

Knowing that he wanted to continue their friendship back in Wellington was a major step and she was looking forward to their return and sharing the city lifestyle. There was so much to do around the inner city and she wanted to introduce him to some of her favourite places. She would be finishing up in Springvale at the end of the week and her project at the museum back home would probably last a little longer. Then she would have to look for another position, but she wouldn't worry about that right now, as part-time work was usually available.

Jason was having similar thoughts as he strode beside Alana. He wanted to get to know her better and then introduce her to his rugby friends. There would be so many experiences to share back in Wellington.

A breeze was coming from the water as they reached the park and Alana pulled her collar up higher to keep out the cold. She stumbled over a rocky patch and Jason grabbed her tightly, taking his time before letting her go. He pushed a strand of hair from her face and kissed her lightly on the lips.

"I've been wanting to do that for a while," he confessed and they laughed and clung to each other, before kissing again. Alana shivered in the crisp night air and put her arms around Jason's waist. "Maybe we should go back where it's warm," she said. "We could share a nightcap up in my room and enjoy the moment."

Jason needed no persuading and it wasn't long before they were back in the warmth of the tavern and climbing almost furtively up the stairs where Alana uncorked a bottle of red wine and produced two small glasses. They sat together on the side of the bed and sipped their drinks, neither wanting to make the first move.

Alana felt shy and awkward. She always seemed to feel this way at the start of a relationship. "I'm not very good at this," she laughed. "But I do want to get to know you better."

Jason seemed just as hesitant. "I want to get to know you too. Let's think about what we will do back in Wellington at the weekend. There are so many places I would like to take you. When were you planning on going back?"

Alana relaxed. "I thought I could probably leave here on Friday afternoon. It won't take me long to pack and say my goodbyes to the Evans. I'll sure miss Jan's cooking next week though. What about yourself?"

Jason still had a few weeks' work in Springvale but could also return to Wellington on Friday so it was decided that he would take the train from the Hutt into the city and meet Alana at the boatshed which was close to her apartment. From there they would let the evening take care of itself.

As Jason had an early start the next morning, they talked for a while and he gave her another hug and kiss as he left the room. They had all week to see each other and neither of them felt like rushing their blossoming friendship. After all, it felt a bit like a holiday romance,

and the test would come when they returned to life in the
city.

Chapter 13

The news of Richard Seddon's visit to Clifton spread through the town like wildfire. Shop keepers dragged out the bunting and ribbons they used to decorate their windows and a large hand written sign 'Clifton Welcomes King Dick' was strung across the road and tied to two telegraph poles. There was an air of excitement in the town as everyone wished to shake the hand of New Zealand's most popular Prime Minister.

He was to arrive by automobile, a very rare sight in the country town and everyone was keen to catch sight of this new contraption which would surely never take over from horse drawn vehicles.

Old Elias shook his head at the thought of the chaos when the timid animals saw the automobile for the very first time. "We will get into town early and tether our horses out of harm's way," he said. His wife Mary agreed. "Perhaps we should take up John Cameron's invitation to have the girls' hair cut and styled. That would be a welcome treat for them," she said.

"I feel it would be unseemly for women to enter a men's barber's shop," was Elias' reply. "But if he has created a suitable interior, maybe I could change my mind." Young Mary and Jean jumped up and down with excitement. To have their hair professionally trimmed and fashioned was something they had never dreamed possible unless they visited the city of Dunedin where beauty shops were becoming quite popular.

Then of course there was the problem of what to wear. Long black dresses and white blouses with a frill were the norm and there were ways of decorating them with a fancy pin, beads or flower arrangement. Boater hats with a bright ribbon would be worn and a pair of sturdy boots to cope with the stony roads and uneven paving. The men just needed trousers, a jacket and clean shirt and no decent man was seen in public without a hat.

The Prime Minister would be in the village for about an hour, listening to speeches from the council and road board and then giving an address of his own, probably with promises of a new paved road and government assistance for the promising wool industry. Elias wanted to ask a question about the future of the lime industry as the district's farmers were querying the use of lime as a fertiliser.

John Cameron and the young barber were thrilled to receive a note from the Gregg family accepting the offer of hair appointments. With such a well respected family gracing their premises it might lead to a new trend in the town. Elias was still a little reluctant as there was only a thin wall between the salon and bath house and the wrong conversation might offend delicate ears.

However, the Greggs set off in good spirits to enjoy the day. It was now early summer and the weather was warm and sunny so there was little need for the pile of blankets that always travelled with the farm cart. Mary was filled with excited anticipation at seeing John Cameron once again and had taken extra pains over her appearance. Her blouse had been ironed to perfection and the straw hat set at a jaunty angle.

The main street was already filled with horse-drawn buggies by the time the Gregg family arrived in Clifton. Elias knew of a field one street back from the town where he could safely tether the horses until their return.

They would be content as long as they had a bag of hay to munch.

Mary and Jean made their way across the grassy field to the stony track and looked around them. "We must go to John's salon at once or we will miss the arrival of the Prime Minister." Mary bustled her sister along, while their mother waited for Elias and William to lead the horses to the fence and tether them. "You two go on ahead," she called to them. "I will meet you at the barber's shop later."

Picking up their long skirts to avoid the rough grass, the pair quickly headed for the main street and threaded their way through the throngs of bystanders already lining up for the first glimpse of Richard Seddon. John Cameron and Nick Postles were both busy when they arrived so they sat on the newly upholstered couch and waited for Nick to finish.

Nick had employed a young woman to help and she welcomed the girls and led Jean to the basin to shampoo her hair. "You just sit on that chair and put your head over the basin," she instructed, after handing Jean a soft towel to hold over her face. The salon had the luxury of warm water from a steam boiler and a large jug of the water was handily placed to rinse off the shampoo.

This was a far cry from heating water on the stove back at the farm and filling the large round basin which was usually placed on a board beside the back door of the house.

As Mary waited nervously for her turn, she looked up to see John Cameron standing in front of her. "I hope you will enjoy our salon," he said. "I have finished my work for the morning and would like you to walk with me as soon as Nick has arranged your hair."

"Thank you. That would be very pleasant," Mary blushed as the words tumbled out. Did this invitation mean that John was interested in getting to know her better? But now the woman was ready to shampoo her hair and she allowed herself to be led to the wash basin. At the same time, Nick was ready for Jean at the barber's chair.

"I would like to try one of the latest styles," he said, as he gently combed the long hair into place and parted it in the middle. First we will shorten your hair a little, then I would like it to softly curl around your face. The rest we will tie back in a loose knot." He picked up the warm crimping iron and began to twirl a few strands around the tongs.

Jean watched herself in the mirror, fascinated by the young barber's skills. She couldn't wait to go out into the street and show off her new look. Her school friends would be most envious.

Soon it was Mary's turn and this time Nick decided on a more sophisticated look, rolling the hair back and off the face, then piling the long tresses on top of her head and pinning them securely. She wasn't quite sure whether she liked the effect, although it did make her appear more elegant. John gave her an approving look and came across from the other side of the room to take her arm and lead her out into the busy street.

Nick closed the salon door and joined the group, looking forward to a welcome afternoon off. The dusty road was by now lined with people, and every vantage point was taken. Soon the cheers could be heard in the distance as the open roadster, flanked by police on horseback came into view.

In the back seat sat the rotund figure of the Prime Minister with Lady Seddon beside him wearing a very large hat trimmed with feathers. Streamers were flung across the road and the cheers were ear-shattering as the cavalcade advanced and stopped outside the town hall where the dignitaries were waiting. Mary clutched John's hand in excitement as he made the most of the opportunity to place a protective arm around her waist.

"This really is a most momentous occasion. Clifton will remember this day for many years to come."

Chapter 14

The rest of the week flew by quickly for Alana with the final photographs being taken at the graveyard and several trips to the local museum to research the history of the area. She and Jason met for dinner in the evenings, but they weren't together long as he had an early start each day, surveying for a new development several kilometres out of town.

Alana was still attracted to John Cameron's grave, with its grassy mound and yellow dandelions. She knew she would continue working on his story back in Wellington and learn more about Clifton, the village where he had lived before moving to Springvale.

She had struck up quite a friendship with Flo Avery at the museum and promised to return and visit her in the near future. She knew she would always have a warm welcome at the Springvale Tavern and would miss the company of Jan and Bruce. "Jason will be with you for a few more weeks and I can come back and see you once my assignment is finished," she promised, after she had packed her belongings into the car and gone back to say her goodbyes.

As she drove away, Alana felt a sense of sadness creep over her. She had enjoyed her time in this small village and returning to the big, busy city left her with a feeling of emptiness. She was also a little nervous about meeting Jason in a different environment. There were so many distractions in Wellington and their relationship had scarcely begun.

"Enough gloom and doom. We'll have a good time tonight and everything will work out great." She said the words aloud to convince herself and grinned as she caught a reflection of her anxious face in the rear vision mirror, then turned onto the highway which would lead her to the city.

****

With her newly arranged hair and John Cameron as her escort, Mary floated through the afternoon, allowing herself to be led to the small tearooms in the village and on to the long wooden verandah out the back where extra tables had been set in readiness for the day's events.

The trim waitress wore a crisp white apron over her long black skirt and took their afternoon tea order. "It'll be along in a moment." She smiled at John and admired Mary's new hair style, asking who had created it. "It was in my very own salon. You will have to come and try out our new premises for the ladies," John beamed. He turned to Mary and took her hand in his. "I think you are about to bring us luck. The ladies will soon be lining up at the door, just you wait and see."

"I certainly hope so. Nick does a very good job and deserves to succeed." Mary replied. "This has been such an exciting afternoon. I want it to go on for ever."

She plucked a piece of fluff from John's suit lapel and blushed as she realised what she had done. The tea trolley was wheeled in at this point and a three-tier plate stand laden with finely cut sandwiches, small meat pies and a cream-filled sponge cake cut into slices was placed on the table.

The waitress placed the cups and teapot with a jug of milk and bowl of sugar alongside the cake stand, and stood back, ready to fill the cups when required. John handed Mary a small white china plate and realizing she was hungry, she helped herself to a ham sandwich and succulent pie.

John took two pies and two sandwiches and nodded to the waitress to pour the tea into the delicate china cups. A little milk and spoon of sugar were added and she re-filled the pot with hot water before going off to serve the next table.

Mary smiled at John in appreciation. She had visited the tearooms a few times with her parents but the whole experience was so much more pleasurable today. She sipped the tea and looked around. A woman at the next table gave her a second look and nodded in her direction. Mary recognised her as one of the stalwarts of the English church.

John lifted a piece of cream sponge onto the cake knife and placed it expertly on her plate. She broke a piece of with a silver cake fork and placed in her mouth, licking the cream from her lips as John looked at her and laughed. "You are very beautiful, young Mary," he said." That touch of cream really sets off the redness of your mouth."

He placed a large piece of cake in his own mouth and wiped away the excess with a cloth napkin. "Mmm. Delicious. I think we should do this more often."

After a second cup of tea and another slice of cake, it was time to leave the tearooms and catch up with the rest of the family who would be anxious to get back to the farm before evening. Mary took John's arm as they walked along the narrow path which had been so crowded earlier. Most of the townspeople had now left to go back to work or return to their homes, the excitement of the day behind them.

"You are welcome to join us for supper," Mary's mother said as John escorted her daughter back to the waiting gig and horses. "You can ride with us and borrow a horse to get you back to town."

John took little persuading and was soon seated alongside Mary and Jean at the back of the cart as the horses jogged along the street, eager to be back on the farm where they could run free after being confined all day in the village.

Jean was envious when she learned that her sister had been entertained at the tearooms. She and Nick had stood together to watch the Prime Minister's speech but Nick had returned to the salon where a few customers were waiting. He had hoped for a free afternoon but that was not to be.

However, he had asked Jean to save a dance for him at the social event to be held at the school at the end of term. That was only a week away, and Jean was looking forward to the holidays even though it would mean more chores to be done around the farm.

****

The sun was going down behind the hills when Alana arrived at the boat shed a little after 5 o'clock. It was just a short stroll, through the museum grounds, from where she lived. Then onto the waterfront which was busy with walkers, board riders and joggers, all out to catch the last of the day's sun.

The boat shed was filling up fast as she looked anxiously around for Jason who would be walking from the train station further along the quay. When she caught sight of him, her heart jumped. She walked towards him and he smiled when he saw her and strode in her direction.

Alana almost skipped along the pier and was soon in his arms. It felt so right to be there.

"How did the train work out? Did you have much of a wait?"

"I was lucky. I just made it in time. The trains are not very frequent from the Hutt at this time of day. Everyone is going the other way." Jason put an arm around her shoulder and they walked along the water's edge until they came to a long wooden seat. "But I'm here now and that's all that matters."

Alana smiled and took Jason's hand. "Let's walk for a while and then decide where to go. There are so many places I want to share with you. I just love the city at this time of night."

"I tend to stay out in the Hutt Valley and catch up with a few mates so you probably know more about Wellington than I do. I usually only come in when there is a rugby match on." They walked by the sheltered waters where the rowing club was out in force with crews of eight and several smaller craft. The water gleamed in the last rays of sunlight, before the shadow of the high-rise buildings filtered out the light.

A few hardy teenagers were diving from the pier and seagulls noisily scrapped over a package of uneaten fish and chips.

A new bar and tavern a little further along the waterfront caught their attention. "I've never been here. Shall we give it a try?" Alana led the way into the quiet interior which was subtly decorated in grey and black with highlights of red on the cushions and wall hangings. They settled themselves on a couch near the window as a wine waiter approached them keen to take their order. A beer and a wine, along with a bowl of nibbles, were brought to their table and Jason raised his glass and smiled at Alana. "Here's to getting to know you."

They drank to that and relaxed in the convivial surroundings. The conversation flowed between them as if they had never been apart, then they left the bar and walked a little further towards the city centre and ate at a Thai restaurant which was one of Alana's favourites. The food was good and the price was reasonable.

Strolling hand in hand through the streets, they mingled with the dozens of students who were celebrating the end of another week of study. They glanced into the boat shed as they headed back along the pier. The noisy crowd was celebrating an out-of-town Wellington rugby win but Alana and Jason walked on by, not needing to be part of the celebrations tonight.

Alana knew they were headed for her flat and that Jason would stay the night. It just seemed like the natural thing to do.

Chapter 15

John Cameron enjoyed another convivial evening in the Gregg household. After supper, Mary was persuaded to accompany him on the piano as he sang a Scottish air and then he entertained them with a humorous verse. His hosts loaned him a sturdy brown mare to ride back to town and he would leave it overnight in the small field behind the salon where his own horse was grazing.

That would be a good excuse to visit Mary the next day when he returned the mare. He poured a small glass of whisky before retiring for the night and sat and thought about the day's events. His living quarters above the salon had always been adequate for his needs but would not be suitable if he ever married. How would he be able to afford a house to rent on the meagre income from his share of the business? He would need to think carefully about another venture to bring in more funds.

He glanced through the pages of the local newspaper that had arrived earlier and noticed a small advertisement for an insurance agency. He put his glass down and looked at the advertisement more carefully. They wanted a local agent for a well-known insurance company with a good rate of commission paid. John knew he had the perfect location for such a venture and decided then and there to word a reply.

He carefully listed his skills and folded the page into a clean white envelope which he would post the next day. Yes, selling insurance should be an easy way to make the extra money he needed.

****

As Alana turned the key in the door of her apartment on the hill she was suddenly conscious of how small and cramped it would seem to Jason. She hadn't had much time to unpack her bags before meeting Jason earlier that evening, and tried to recall what sort of state her room would be in.

Jason was intrigued at the narrow steps leading straight up from the street to the door. Many Wellington houses were perched on steep hillsides at impossible angles which must have needed a high level of skill in the early days of the city's development. "This is so handy to everything, but where do you keep your car?" Alana explained that there was a garage behind the building with a shared driveway, but turning around to come back down was no easy matter. "It's just as well my car is so small," she said.

Once inside, she hurriedly picked up the pile of clothes which covered the sofa and apologised for the state of the apartment. Jason just laughed and held her hand. He headed her for the sofa and took her in his arms before she could make a start on the crowded bench top. "It's perfect. Just leave everything the way it is." He kissed her soundly then walked across to the refrigerator to inspect its contents. He took a bottle of cool white wine from the shelf and looked around for glasses. Alana pointed to the cupboard above the microwave and he produced two goblets which he partly filled.

"So this is how you city dwellers live. Very cosy, that's for sure."

"It's plenty big enough for one." Alana blushed. "A burly fellow like you would probably need a lot more space." She sipped the wine and moved closer. "I can't offer you any food I'm afraid. I need to go shopping in the morning."

"I think we have done very well already." Jason put down his glass and drew Alana into his arms. She relaxed and placed her wine on the coffee table beside the sofa. "As I said, this is very cosy." He stroked her hair back from her forehead and she leaned back against the soft cushion. His kiss grew more intense and she could feel her body responding to his touch. "I think I need another drink." Alana sat up and straightened her clothing. "Then perhaps we should get more comfortable."

****

When John walked down the stairs to the salon the next day his mind was buzzing with possibilities. He had an important evening coming up at the school prize giving where he hoped to recruit more young men to join his fitness studio. Then if he was able to secure the insurance agency there would be the chance of a larger income.

At present he held his physical culture evenings in the local hall and seniors paid one guinea per quarter in advance to join. Youths under 17 were charged 12 shillings and sixpence and it was in this group that he was having his biggest success. "No expensive apparatus is required to enable you to acquire a splendidly developed body, with muscles as firm and strong as steel," his advertisements claimed.

As it was Saturday, the shop was open in the morning with Nick lining up a few customers for hair cuts and beard trims. John was kept busy with sports massage and supervising the baths, but once the customers left he wasted no time in saddling his horse as well as the borrowed mare and soon he was on his way to the Gregg farm leading the mare. He was hoping to invite Mary for a ride and then a walk alongside the stream that ran through the Gregg property. It was a beautiful autumn afternoon and the trees were already taking on their colourful mantle before the cold of winter set in.

Mary came out to help him with the horses and soon they were riding companionably side by side towards the back of the property. She wore a long skirt and rode side saddle although she admitted that at times she preferred to ride in trousers like a boy when her parents weren't around. The green of the fields contrasted vividly with the white of the lime deposits and the spectacular countryside reminded him of his own family farm just a few miles away.

Once they reached the farm boundary, they halted the horses and dismounted in a grove of shady trees. John soon had the horses tethered and wasted no time in taking Mary in his arms and kissing her tenderly at first and then more persuasively. Her first reaction was to step back but she was determined to act in an adult way and found herself responding. She allowed him to touch her face and as his hand began to trace the outline of her arm she trembled.

Before she knew it, John had placed his heavy overcoat on the ground and sat her gently down. He produced a flask of whisky from his pocket and gave her a drop in a small cup. She smelt it and tasted it with her tongue but the unaccustomed strength made her gasp and she was reluctant to drink another drop. John poured himself a small dram and drank it slowly, trailing his hand along her body.

His kisses became more urgent as his hand caressed her and she was lowered to the ground with the hardness of his body pressing against her. Mary felt a ridge of ground under her spine and moved to a more comfortable position. With John's hand beginning to move up her leg, she grew apprehensive. She had not anticipated the strength of his muscles and tried to move way.

"I'm sorry. It's just that I want you so much," he muttered in her ear. Not wanting to frighten her, he withdrew his hand and caressed her hair which had escaped the coiffure and now hung over her shoulder. He held her tight and a great shudder came over his body as he tensed against her, then he rolled away and lay still.

Mary got to her feet and straightened her clothing. There was not much she could do about her hair which was now loose around her face. John sat up awkwardly and clasped his hands around his knees.

"You are much too beautiful, my dear. I find it difficult to keep my feelings for you under control. But never fear, I would do nothing to harm you."

He got to his feet and took her hand and they walked along the stream's edge and sat down in a patch of sunlight. Mary felt shy and awkward after the encounter. She wanted to spend time with John Cameron but was not yet ready for his advances.

"We must return before darkness falls," she said primly. "My parents will be anxious if I am away too long." She led the way back to where their horses were tethered and tightened the girth on the saddle before mounting her mare. They trotted back along the track beside the stream and cantered over the fields towards the homestead as the sun set behind the distant hills.

John cursed himself for his clumsy advances. Mary was young and totally inexperienced and he knew he would have to gain her confidence before getting any closer. He kicked his horse and set off in a gallop towards the house. By the time Mary caught up, he had unlatched the gate and held it open for her to ride through. Her cheeks were flushed and her hair disheveled, but the ride across the farm would account for that.

"Please thank your parents for their hospitality and I hope to see you again soon. I'd better ride back into town while I can still see the road."

"Yes, well goodbye for now. And I would like to see you again. Maybe the school prize giving next week would be a good opportunity." Mary rode towards the stable where she would unsaddle her mare before returning to the house to face her parents.

Her mind was in a state of confusion. She felt a great attraction for John but had been frightened by the intensity of his love making. She would meet him in company from now on and not spend too much time with him alone.

Chapter 16

In the early hours of the morning Alana woke and re-alised that Jason lay beside her in the Queen sized bed which took up most of the space in the small room. She stretched over and touched the bare skin on his back and he rolled over and put his arms around her. Their love-making had been frantic and hurried the night before and at the last minute he had reached for a condom before entering her.

This time they took their time, caressing each other un-til he was ready to enter her again. She hugged him tightly and when he tried to withdraw she held him with her knees as they rocked in harmony and exploded to-gether.

"I'm sorry. That wasn't meant to happen." Jason tried to apologise, but Alana only laughed and held him more tightly.

"It's okay. It was my fault, and I don't really care. I'm glad we waited and now I don't want you to ever go away." They fell back to sleep, satiated and content in each other's arms. They had a whole weekend to be to-gether before Jason returned to Springvale.

When they woke again the sun was struggling through the clouds and the Wellington wind was scurrying the autumn leaves in all directions. After a cup of coffee and a slice of toast Jason walked to the corner store to pick up a newspaper as Alana tidied away the clothes that had ended up in a heap on the floor.

"It's a bit too cool to walk around the city today. Would you like me to drive you back to the Hutt and show me where you hang out?" Alana was keen to see the apartment where Jason lived and take the opportunity to get to know him better.

"That sounds like a good plan but I warn you, it is a real bachelor's pad. We will need to stop off and buy some food and maybe you should bring some gear and stay the night."

Alana didn't take any persuading, so her small car was soon packed and they were heading along the highway towards the valley where the city had sprawled over the years. Jason's grandparents had once lived in the Hutt but the property had long been taken over for state housing. "It's hard to imagine that this was where the old farm was with the Hutt River running along the boundary, but see, the original house is still standing."

Sure enough the rough-cast concrete house stood out among the wooden and brick homes which had been erected during an earlier housing boom.

They drove past sports fields where hundreds of children were involved in their various sporting codes although the winter season had scarcely begun. Alana knew that netball and rugby drew the biggest crowds while soccer was gaining in popularity with mixed teams of boys and girls.

A visit to the supermarket resulted in a large quantity of plastic bags being piled into the boot of the car as Jason offered to barbecue some steaks for dinner that evening. Baked potatoes with sour cream and chives and a salad were also on the menu, followed by frozen apple pie and custard. And for breakfast they had chosen eggs and bacon and fresh orange juice.

Jason's apartment was in a block of four, each with an attached garage and fenced back yard. An assortment of children's toys filled the yard next door and two small faces peered over the fence as Alana's car pulled into the driveway.

"Hi kids," Jason called. "How are things?" The children called out in reply until they were taken inside by their mother. "They're good kids. Their mother is from the Philippines and their father is a Kiwi," Jason explained. "I feel a bit sorry for her as her English is not very good and she has few friends in the area."

He opened the door and they went inside. The rooms were dark and stuffy with a small kitchen out the back and a lounge in the front. Two bedrooms ran off a hallway with a bathroom at the end. One of the rooms was obviously a storeroom, with boxes and books covering every surface.

Alana was pleased to find that the kitchen was clean and tidy and she packed the food into the fridge and cupboard as Jason opened windows and rolled up the shades. She took her bag into the bedroom and pulled up the blind. A flowering tree covered most of the window shutting out the sunlight.

Jason brewed a coffee and turned on the television. A replay of the previous evening's rugby match was in full swing. Alana wasn't much of a rugby fan so she picked up the newspaper and skimmed the headlines.

Observing this, Jason put their cups on the bench and suggested they pack a lunch and go for a drive. "There is quite a bit of history on the fringes of town. One of my relatives owned the first timber mill with its own water wheel. There is still evidence of the remains if I can remember where to look."

Alana agreed and between them they boiled eggs, filled some bread rolls with meat and salad, packed a bottle of wine and glasses into a carry bag and took along a selection of fruit. Jason drove his utility this time and Alana was able to take in the scenery. At first the streets were lined with older houses, then they drove through some new suburbs. It wasn't long before they were on the edge of town and a road led up the hill to what looked like an old quarry at the top.

"The original mill was somewhere in that scrub country beside a waterfall which ran the water wheel." Jason pulled up at the end of the road and looked around. "We can follow that fence line and see if we can find the stream." They stumbled across long grass and between gorse bushes and sure enough a narrow stream wound its way across the field. "The water fall must be up at the top of that hill."

It had been many years since Jason last visited the area and he wasn't sure whether there would be anything left of the old mill site. They climbed a fence and made their way to the top of the hill. From there a fine view took in the town below and surrounding countryside. "The original homestead was just below the mill. I've seen photos and it was a very substantial dwelling with many rooms. It took quite a large staff to run it."

"Was there a large family?" Alana was curious. "They must have been very rich to afford all those servants."

"Back in those days, help wasn't expensive and every high class household employed cooks and maids. I'm sure the same was true for many families living in those times."

By now they had reached the top of the hill and sat down on a grassy slope to catch their breath. "Enough history lessons for today. Let's just enjoy out time together. Come here and give me a kiss." Jason reached out for Alana and pulled her down on the grass beside him.

They lay in each other's arms with the sun shining down on them, protected by the tall grass and wild flowers blooming in the field. "This is very nice, but I think we should try to find that waterfall," Alana was anxious not to have a repeat of this morning's unprotected love making. If this persisted she would be visiting her doctor next week for contraception advice.

"You're probably right." Jason reluctantly got to his feet. "We'll follow the stream to the edge of the hillside and the waterfall should still be there." Sure enough the narrow stream disappeared over the bank but instead of a waterfall, a rusty pipe carried most of the water to a nearby trough.

"That trickle would hardly keep a mill running." Alana was surprised. "I guess if there's a lot of rain some of the water would still spill over the edge." The brambles and gorse bushes hid any sign of a building in the valley below so they headed back to where the utility was parked.

Jason looked around the clearing at the end of the road and spied a flat rock which would make a handy table. "We may as well have lunch here and then we could drive out to the winery and see whether it's open. You never know with some of those places."

Alana didn't mind what they did today. She felt relaxed and happy as she helped carry the lunch containers over to the rock. Opening the wicker picnic basket she found a red plastic table cloth which covered the plates and glasses.

Christmas bells and sprigs of holly were a little incongruous at this time of year but the cloth was soon spread over the mossy rock. Jason took the wine bottle from the cooler and poured it into two plastic glasses. He had produced two folding chairs from the back of the utility and soon their picnic was set up. The wine was cool and the bread rolls were delicious. Alana peeled an egg and ate it with the roll. "You could go to the best restaurant in town, but this lunch tastes as good as any."

They sat in silence. The only sounds were the chirping of birds and the rustle of the breeze through the grass and scrub. Alana and Jason were in no hurry to pack up and leave. Alana lay back on the soft grass as Jason sat on a mound and took in the view of the valley below.

"I suppose we could make a move and drive to the winery," he said at last. Alana stood and stretched her arms above her head. "I guess so but this is such a lovely place."

Soon the containers were returned to the utility and Jason drove slowly back to the main road and further out into the countryside. He patted Alana on the knee. "Enjoying your day out?" He glanced in her direction. "You know I am," she smiled back.

Chapter 17

Mary was looking forward to the school prize giving with a mixture of excitement and apprehension. On the one hand she wanted to see John Cameron again, but she still felt nervous in his company. Jean was busy rehearsing musical items with the pupils but was also thinking of the dancing to follow the handing out of the prizes. Nick had asked her to save a dance for him and that would be an improvement on the clumsy boys who were in the senior class.

Several of them were leaving at the end of the term to take up positions on the local farms, but she was quite happy to remain at school as long as she could be trained for her teaching certificate. She was already preparing many of the lessons for the younger pupils, supervised by the school master.

"What are you planning on wearing on Friday night?" Mary asked as she looked through the wardrobe in despair. "I'm so tired of the same dresses and as for that black skirt, I think it has seen better days." She pulled out a blue taffeta dress with ruffles around the neckline.

"You could sew some new lace on that one. I'm sure our mother has plenty of trimmings in her sewing basket." Jean knew she would be expected to wear a plain skirt and white blouse befitting her role as pupil teacher. She would allow her hair to hang freely to her waist, however.

The sewing basket was brought out and the contents spilled onto the table. "You are right. This cream lace edging will be perfect along the ruffles. I'll work on it straight away." Mary replaced the contents of the basket and took out a needle and thread from the drawer of the sewing machine. The new treadle machine was her mother's pride and joy and many a fine garment had been created since its arrival.

As it was Jean's turn to milk the house cow, Mary was left to transform her dress and day dream about the forthcoming event.

****

John Cameron was also busy preparing for the big night. It was an important occasion for him as his pupils would be putting on a display of the various feats of strength and he was hoping to impress the audience with his own expertise. The first exhibition was a local competition for untrained men, the winner to be the man who could lift a 57 pound weight most times with one hand. Then a number of his senior pupils would try to lift more than 120 pounds.

 He also promoted the sale of dumb bells, guaranteed to last a lifetime, and finish off with his familiar sales pitch: "Young men, if you only knew the increase of health, strength and physical activity my system of training will give you, you would not delay one day longer." He could usually count on a number of new pupils each time he organised this type of performance.

Once the demonstration was over, he could concentrate on the entertainment. He had been asked to sing one song and knew an encore would probably be requested. Then he would be free to seek out the young woman who was constantly on his mind. There would be the opportunity to share supper and dance together as the night went on.

His best suit had been cleaned and pressed and a white shirt hung in the wardrobe ready for the occasion. A grey waist coat and a black bow tie would complete the effect. He twisted the ends of his waxed moustache and slicked his dark hair back in a fashionable style. John didn't want to look like a Dandy, but his amateur stage performances had taught him how to make the best of his appearance.

He would also write an account of the evening which would be published in the city papers. Yes, there were many strings to John Cameron's bow.

****

It took about half an hour for Jason and Alana to reach the winery which was tucked into a sheltered valley along a winding country road. "I don't know how anyone finds their way out here. This place must be the area's most guarded secret." Alana was surprised at the remoteness so close to the city. A small sign on the side of the road pointed to the winery and Jason drove through the gate and along the dusty metalled track.

Grape vines had been planted in rows all through the valley and clusters of small red fruit could be seen through the white netting which had been placed over the vines. "The birds would soon eat the whole crop if they got a chance," explained Jason. "When it's time to harvest the grapes, all the owners' friends and relatives converge on the property to help out. They finish off with a barbecue and a great party I believe."

"That sounds like a lot of fun. I wouldn't mind helping out with that." Alana smiled at the thought. A day in the sun picking grapes and then a wine party could be an interesting experience.

Jason stopped the vehicle in the parking lot beside a tin shed and they made their way into the dark interior. Barrels and crates were stacked all around them and a large golden Labrador strolled towards them wagging her tail.

There was no other sign of life however, so they wandered along a track that led through the rows of grape vines. The sun now shone brightly and the vines offered little shade. The sound of a motor attracted their attention and a quad bike came into view driven by a woman wearing a large straw sunhat.

She waved when she saw them and drove back to the tin shed, the Labrador following.

"Sorry you had to wait. My husband is in town and there are jobs to be done."

She disappeared into a small wash room and came out minus the hat, her dark hair tied back in a shaggy pony tail. "Hi. I'm Erica and welcome to Sunnyvale Wines. Our vines are now 10 years old and we make a small amount of Merlot on the property."

She took a bottle from an ancient cupboard and poured a quantity into three plastic glasses. Alana sipped her wine slowly. Merlot was not one of her favourites. Jason and Erica appeared to be enjoying their sample, however, and Erica refilled their glasses with an older vintage.

Alana wandered off and looked around the shed, taking in the old implements and relics from the past which were hanging from the walls. This had the makings of a country museum, she thought.

"Has this property been in your family for long? It must have quite a history."

"My husband's grandfather first farmed the property, milking a few cows and raising pigs. But it is much too small for a dairy farm these days," Erica explained.

Jason paid for a bottle of wine and soon they were back in the utility and heading for the city. "I know of a nice little tavern where we could have a drink on the way home," he said. Alana was feeling shy about going back to his house but wanted the day to last forever.

"Sounds good. Then we can barbecue the steaks when we get back."

The tavern was in a small village similar to Springvale and Alana almost expected to see Bruce and Jan Evans behind the bar. It would seem strange not to be returning there on Sunday, especially when Jason was going back without her. Jason seemed to know the tavern owner and the tall blonde waitress who brought their drinks.

He introduced Alana and they settled down at a table close to a cosy gas fire which warmed up the room. This was Jason's world and Alana was curious to learn more.

The cool white wine was more to Alana's taste and she soon relaxed as they shared a bowl of hot chips which Jason had ordered. The sun was already low in the sky and the breeze was cool as they left the tavern and made their way back to Jason's house and a whole night together.

* * * * * * * * * * * * * * * * *

The evening was going well for John Cameron. His pupils had thrilled the crowd with their weight-lifting feats and a number of the older boys were eager to join his classes. His song had been followed by a humorous recitation which he had written and he smiled in Mary's direction as he acknowledged the applause.

He had managed to sit next to her during the meal and Nick had squashed in beside young Jean who pretended to ignore him. As soon as the dishes had been cleared away, several men made short work of moving the tables and it was time for the dancing to begin. Mary was happy with the way she looked in the taffeta dress. The new lace was most becoming and her hair was wound into a fashionable knot.

Her dance programme had been filled, with John Cameron claiming the supper waltz and the important last dance. It would have been impolite to turn down a number of other young men who were seeking her attention, but it was only John who attracted her interest.

The first waltz was followed by a sedate march and then a lively polka had everyone up on their feet. Mary could see her parents dancing sedately on the far side of the room while the younger men were mostly clumsy and ungainly as they tried to master the steps.

When it came to the supper dance Mary was happy to be in the arms of John who proved to be an excellent dancer. It was some time since they had eaten, so the plates of sandwiches and cakes were soon demolished, along with cold lemon drink and cups of tea.

"Mary my dear, I would love to escort you home but I don't think your parents would approve. Maybe you could ride into town during the week and we could meet up and picnic together." Mary smiled and looked into John's eyes.

"That would be very pleasant," she said. "I'll ride in on Monday and meet you around noon." She relaxed in his arms as he twirled her around the room, oblivious of the other young men who had been seeking her attention. Tonight she was with John and that was all that mattered.

Chapter 18

When Alana woke in Jason's bed she wondered at first where she was. The sight of unfamiliar walls and curtains was followed by the realisation that Jason was no longer beside her.

She sat up abruptly, but heard sounds of cooking in the kitchen as well as the delicious aroma of bacon frying on the stove. She stretched and yawned. Life had taken a turn for the better as she recalled the fun of barbecuing the steak and tossing the salad and enjoying a few glasses of wine before they had headed for the bedroom the night before.

She was a little hazy about what had followed but felt very relaxed about the outcome. Jason looked into the room and saw that she was awake. "Breakfast is almost ready," he said. "Get your body out of that bed and come and join me."

Alana laughed as she fumbled for her robe and made her way to the bathroom. She would shower later as right now she was hungry and ready to enjoy whatever Jason served up for her. A glass of chilled orange juice for starters followed by crispy bacon, fried eggs and tomato on fingers of toast. This was every bit as good as life back at Springvale and she felt thoroughly spoiled.

Jason had already picked up the morning newspaper and had scanned the headlines while he prepared breakfast. "Not much going on today. Except the Wellington Hurricanes won last night against Auckland Blues."

By now Alana knew that Jason was referring to the latest round of rugby and was happy for Jason's sake that his favourite team was on a winning streak. This was all part of the new world she was experiencing.

As Jason had to return to Springvale later in the afternoon they decided to spend the day in Wellington then Alana would return to her own apartment. She wasn't looking forward to that after such a great time in Jason's company but knew she had more work to do on her museum project once he had gone.

There was still much to discover about the mysterious John Cameron and she was anxious to continue the search for answers.

****

Monday got off to a slow start at the salon in Clifton and John Cameron had plenty of time to prepare for the much anticipated visit from young Mary Gregg who had charmed him even more at the school dance. What a beautiful young woman she was and he knew that she had feelings for him as well. He was a little concerned that he was twice her age but knew that many men in his part of the world courted much younger women.

Nick was working on a new sign for the ladies' hairdressing salon, hoping to attract the local women into what had always been a man's domain. He had enjoyed the evening with young Jean but knew he would have stiff competition to capture her interest.

The accommodation above the salon was comfortable but John was worried that it would not be good enough to entertain a young woman. He thought a picnic on the river bank would be more suitable and had packed an assortment of sandwiches, made by the local tea shop, and cold beer as well as a bottle of lemonade.

His horse was ready to be saddled once Mary arrived and they would ride together to one of his favourite places where the stream flowed over a small waterfall beside a smooth grassy area ideal for their picnic.

It was just before noon when he heard the sound of horse's hooves outside the shop and he rushed out to greet Mary who dismounted to join him on the rough pavement. She waited while he saddled his horse and tied the picnic bag to his saddle and then they rode off towards the track which led to the river.

At first thick bush grew alongside the track and the horses walked in single file to dodge the high branches. After a short time they came to a clearing where the grass was grazed by a herd of wild deer. The river was just beyond the clearing with grass and low fern growing right down to the water's edge.

John occasionally came to this place to swim or sit on the bank with a fishing rod although the fresh water fish were not good eating and he usually threw them back. They tethered each horse to a low branch with enough rope to let them munch on the tender grass, and John carried the sack of food and placed it in a hollow in the bank. The shade of the ferns would keep it cool until they were ready to eat.

Mary sat gingerly on the edge of the rug which had been spread over the grass, while John lay on his back looking up at the cotton wool clouds which floated overhead. For a time neither of them spoke.

The sound of the water falling over the rocks was almost hypnotic and soon Mary had taken off her hat and was leaning back on one elbow. "Isn't this a great way to

118

spend a morning?" John turned towards her. "That pool looks very tempting don't you think?"

Mary shuddered at the thought of the cold water and the possibility of eels lurking in its depths. "Not for me. But you go ahead if you wish."

"Perhaps another time. I'll pour us a refreshing drink instead." John poured a container of beer for himself and some lemonade with a small dash of the ale which he handed to Mary. He raised his glass. "Here's to our friendship and many happy days to come," he said and sat down, leaning his back against a tree.

Mary moved to a more comfortable position with her legs dangling over the bank. Her skirt was pulled up and she had removed her sturdy riding boots. She took a sip of the ale and smiled at John. "This is very refreshing. I haven't been to this place before. There is another pool on our farm that we used as a swimming hole when we were much younger. But it's too much trouble when you have to wear so many clothes. And my hair takes so long to dry."

John looked admiringly at her glossy locks which had escaped from the loose knot. "You have very beautiful hair. I would like to see it down around your shoulders."

"I suppose there is no harm in that as no-one is here to see us." Mary pulled the hair clip from the knot and her hair cascaded down around her face. She pushed it back over her shoulders and took another sip of ale.

"My mother was a little upset that I wouldn't be there to help with the laundry today. It is a heavy job for her to do alone. But she seemed happy enough that I would be in your company. I think she respects you and supports our friendship."

"I will have to make sure I continue to please her. And you as well. I really enjoy being with you and would like to ask your parents' consent to court you," John reached out and took Mary's hand, unsure what her reaction would be.

"I'm a little too young to be courted but the suggestion pleasures me. I will turn 18 in three months' time and then I'm sure there would be no objections." Mary squeezed his hand and then moved away a little, straightening her skirt. She felt shy and vulnerable in his presence but her heart was racing and her hand trembled.

"We will wait until nearer your birthday and then I will approach your parents. And now, let's eat these delicious sandwiches before they are spoiled." He brought out the bag of sandwiches and they inspected the selection which included egg, beef and ham on fresh brown bread.

They ate their fill and lay back on the rug, side by side but not touching. John was being careful not to get too close or the temptation would be too great. He had waited this long and could be patient a little longer.

****

As the time drew nearer to Jason's departure for Springvale, Alana felt despondent. She was really enjoying his company and knew she would be lonely once he had gone. But there was still work to do on her museum project and this would keep her busy until he returned on Friday.

Back in her small hillside apartment she decided to pull out all her notes and collate the information she had on John Cameron. Newspaper cuttings, photographs, notes on the saw mill and most important of all, the cemetery record and photos of his lonely grave were soon spread out on the dining table.

She was still puzzled about the change in John Cameron's circumstances that brought him from Clifton in the South Island to Springvale in the north. What had made him change his occupation from fitness instructor, salon owner and journalist to that of sawmill worker?

She had almost finished listing the inscriptions on the old graves ready for the museum project and she was being paid for another two weeks to come up with some accompanying information on the Springvale area. The story of John Cameron would be a major part of the assignment.

Alana looked again at the photos she had found in the old newspaper. The man smiling back at her must have been very handsome in his day. The slicked back hair, waxed moustache and ornate waistcoat would have attracted many young women she would have thought.

Yet the lonely grave in that old forestry settlement told a different story. She searched through the birth register for the name Cameron around the time he would have worked in Clifton. On May 12, 1913, a son had been born to a John Cameron and Mary. A month later, a daughter was born to parents John and Catherine. It was all a bit confusing.

Perhaps there would be more information in the town of Clifton. She would contact their local museum in the morning and someone there might be able to provide the answers she was looking for. That night she fell asleep with John Cameron's story very much on her mind. Images of a handsome man in a silver waistcoat kept haunting her. One moment he would be standing there and then he would disappear.

Chapter 19

It was 10 o'clock the next morning before Alana left her flat and walked along the waterfront to the maritime museum where she could talk to one of the committee members about completing the cemetery project.

Estelle Jones was working on some files in the back room and greeted Alana enthusiastically. "We are looking forward to seeing the rest of your work," she said. "We have been impressed with what you have done so far."

"There isn't too much more to do as far as the graves are concerned, but further details arc hard to come by for the mysterious John Cameron."

"If we order a death certificate, that would give us his family details and possibly whether he had any children. Would you like to do that now?"

Alana couldn't believe she had overlooked this source of information. "I have the cemetery record but the death certificate is likely to tell us more," she said. "How stupid of me not to have thought of it."

"Family research is our business," Estelle answered. "We learn to use every tool at our disposal."

They soon found the death records site on the Internet and typed in the details for John Cameron. A number of possibilities showed up but the most likely was a man who had died two days before the recorded burial. The certificate was soon ordered and paid for by the museum.

"I think your story will be a worthwhile one as a record of life at the time. It makes it more interesting to have a real person to attach it to, so keep working on it." Estelle bustled off to deal with a query from the young woman behind the front desk and Alana took the opportunity to enjoy the exhibits on display at this very interesting museum which featured the early days of Wellington and history of events on the treacherous Cook Strait.

Back at her flat two hours later she wondered how Jason's day was going and sent him a text message which was answered a short time later. "Find an excuse to come back to Springvale. You can stay with me."

Alana smiled but knew she had little time left to complete the project and being with Jason would be a distraction. It would be great to go back to the tavern, however. Maybe she could find a reason to visit Springvale next week.

****

Mary's mother noticed her happy mood when she returned from the picnic with John Cameron. "You know Mr Cameron is much older and more experienced that you," she cautioned. "I hope you are acting in a way a young lady should."

Mary smiled. John had been a perfect gentleman at all times and she was sure that would continue. "I feel safer with him than some of those loutish boys from the school. I'm sure he would not treat me badly."

"Your father and I are a little worried at his ability to maintain a wife and home. He would hardly make a decent living from those weight lifting lessons, and is seems that young Nick is doing most of the work in the salon." Mary was concerned for her elder daughter.

"We're just friends, mother. Marriage has not been considered." Mary stood up and left the room hurriedly. She didn't want to let her mother know she cared for this man. Why couldn't she be 10 years older, then the age difference wouldn't be a problem.

The older Mary continued rolling out the pastry on the wooden bench top. It was such a short time since her daughter had been safely in the classroom and she wasn't ready to admit that she was now a young woman. Perhaps they should send her to work in Dunedin at her sister's haberdashery store. She would meet more people her own age in the city.

Up in the bedroom she shared with her sister Jean, Mary lay on the narrow bed and then decided to write John Cameron a note thanking him for the day's outing and the picnic lunch. It could be delivered by the rural mail man the next day.

She found a sheet of paper and an envelope and was soon busy composing the note, which she hid under the pillow when Jean returned from milking.

"Playing ladies, I see," her sister chided her. "First you're out with your gentleman friend and now you are resting while the rest of us do all the work." Jean pulled a clean dress from the wardrobe and disappeared to wash in the tin tub outside the back door.

Mary felt a little guilty but pulled out the note and continued writing. She would put it out in the mail box later in the evening ready for the mail man to call. She felt a quiver of excitement as she read the words she had written and wondered what John's response would be.

****

When John Cameron received the note from young Mary he smiled at her enthusiastic words. He was frustrated that it was still three months until her 18th birthday, as he was keen to progress the friendship into a deeper relationship. Perhaps in the meantime it would be wise to meet her only when there were other people around. He knew she would shy away like a young filly from any lovemaking at this stage.

"Things are quiet in the salon this week," he said to Nick who was sitting in the barber's chair waiting for someone to come through the door. "It seems as though the customers are not exactly flocking to the door and as for the bath house, hardly anyone is using it."

Nick looked worried as well. He had heard that more people were heating water in their own homes with boilers fuelled by the new fangled cooking stoves. With the advent of bathrooms in the better dwellings, there would soon be little call for a public bath house.

He was loathe to share the information with John as he was not involved with that side of the business. It would suit him fine to take over the ownership of the barber's shop which was more profitable and he was hoping that this would be possible soon.

John was also worried at the failure to enroll any more weightlifting students following his demonstration at the school. Normally these evenings resulted in an influx of new members. He realised that he was coping financially as a bachelor, but would not be able to support a wife and family unless business improved. Perhaps it was time to try his luck in the city like his brother James who was employed at a major museum and art gallery. He was able to provide a home for his wife and children.

John Cameron was not the only one feeling the effects of the downturn in the economy. Prices for wool and meat were low so the landowners were not spending as much money in the stores and all the shop owners were complaining at the lack of trade.

****

The atmosphere in Wellington was buzzing as the city prepared for a major art festival which brought many thousands of visitors to the area. Alana had managed to buy tickets for a new play on Saturday night and hoped that Jason would enjoy it. The theatre was a short distance away and was known for its high quality entertainment.

She wasn't sure about Jason's cultural tastes but would invite him to stay over at her flat for a late supper afterwards. She decided to text Angela and see whether they could catch up some time during the week. She had been neglecting her friend lately and felt badly about it.

After buying a few fresh supplies from the supermarket, Alana was soon back home and ready to complete her cemetery listings. She printed out the grave inscriptions with the accompanying photographs and assembled them in a folder ready to present to the museum.

She searched Papers Past once more, especially the Bruce Herald in the Otago area for more clues to the life of John Stirling Cameron. She entered the names of the local schools in the district along with the name and was soon rewarded.

School prizegivings and advertisements for John's business ventures made interesting reading. He had certainly been a popular entertainer and his demonstrations of strength and weight lifting appeared to have been well received.

Then a small news item really caught her eye.

A very pleasant evening was enjoyed recently when the engagement was announced between Miss Mary Gregg, elder daughter of Elias and Mary Gregg of Clifton, and

John Cameron, second son of Margaret and the late Donald Cameron also of Clifton. Dancing was enjoyed in the barn at the Gregg family home followed by a delicious supper. Many gifts and good wishes were bestowed on the happy couple. The celebration coincided with Miss Gregg's 18th birthday.

Alana almost shouted aloud at the discovery. So John Cameron had been engaged to Mary Gregg, but there was a big difference in their ages. What had happened to take him to the mill town of Springvale so soon after this announcement? She was looking forward to receiving the death certificate which might reveal some answers.

She checked her phone for a reply from Angela. Yes, she would like to come to the apartment that evening and could catch up over dinner. Alana sent back a reply. She had so much news to share with her friend and a meal at home would be the best option.

A packet of marinated pork steaks was rescued from the freezer along with some convenient frozen mashed potato. What would her mother say if she knew Alana was resorting to frozen potato? Well, what she didn't know wouldn't hurt her. Steamed broccoli would make up for her lapse, Alana decided, and she knew that Angela would bring over her favourite dessert.

Alana had been so busy that she had little time to consider her next job. Where would she find work once the Springvale project was completed? Having a degree didn't guarantee employment and she was getting used to taking up short term positions.

Something always seemed to crop up when she needed it and up until now she had been prepared to travel from Wellington when an opportunity arose, as long as accommodation was provided. But would she want to move away just when she and Jason were getting to know each other?

Chapter 20

The rest of the week passed quickly and soon it was Friday and time for Jason to return from Springvale. Alana felt a bubble of excitement as she waited for him to negotiate the steep driveway behind the apartment. There was just room to park his vehicle on a flat area with a steep brick retaining wall behind it.

After a week apart, her nervousness had returned but as soon as she was back in his arms she was content. There was a lot of news to catch up on. Work was progressing well back in Springvale and should be completed in a couple of weeks. Jason wasn't sure where his next job would take him but there was always an opening for a surveyor.

"It's great to be back. I don't really care what happens next. We're together now and that's all that matters." He gave her a huge hug and they sat together enjoying a cool wine before they ventured down to the waterfront, the theatre and the play.

The small restaurant which was part of the theatre offered an adequate meal and then they found their seats and sat back to enjoy the play, a comedy which both Alana and Jason enjoyed.

Walking hand in hand back to the small apartment on the hill they passed by many people enjoying an evening stroll along the waterfront, then crossed the road and climbed the steps up to Alana's home. From there they could glimpse the harbour, the museum and the people walking along the waterfront below.

"This is quite a view. You would need a fortune to buy one of these houses." Jason was impressed. "You're right. Angela's family once owned a whole street of houses along the bay. She would like to own just one of them now."

Alana served up a dish of water melon cooled with a spoonful of ice cream. "There's coffee to follow," she said. They sat in silence as they enjoyed the dessert. Jason helped clear the few dishes and then they fell into each other's arms on the couch as they watched the late night television. Their enjoyable weekend was just beginning.

****

After John had received Mary's note he didn't hasten to reply. Perhaps he should slow things down a little while he assessed his prospects. He realised he was in no position to offer a viable marriage to Mary at this stage.

Over the next few days he thought more about his situation. Maybe it was time to hand over the barber's shop to young Nick and work out his future more clearly. He could join a newspaper in the city, writing social gossip and describing in detail the dresses the ladies were wearing. Except if he left anyone out he was in big trouble.

The weightlifting classes were never intended to be a money making venture and the insurance agency had moved its business out of town. It was probably time to seek his fortune elsewhere.

In the meantime he accepted an invitation to lunch at the Gregg household the following week. That should prove to be a pleasant afternoon as he entertained the family with a number of songs, accompanied by Mary on the piano.

Although the family welcomed him, John felt uneasy. Elias Gregg was questioning him on the state of business in the town and Mary was somewhat subdued. The easy relationship they had enjoyed seemed to have changed.

As he was leaving, he found himself alone with Mary. "Are your folks having second thoughts about us? I don't feel as welcome as I did before."

"I think they are worried about the difference in our ages. Don't worry about it. They will be most happy for us to be together once I turn 18. Only just over two months to go." She smiled and turned her face towards him. He brushed his lips on her's and then gave her a deeper kiss.

"I'm sure everything will work out. We will just be patient until your birthday and then it will be a great celebration." Then he took his leave and rode his horse back along the country road to the village. As he approached the tavern, a number of his friends were sitting out on the long verandah. "We haven't seen much of you lately, John Cameron. Are you out with your fancy woman?" they teased.

John turned his horse loose in the small pasture at the rear of the hotel and joined them. What was the point of worrying about tomorrow when there were plenty of good times to be enjoyed today?

He bought a handle of the locally brewed beer and sat on the long bench out on the porch. Yes, this was the life. Enjoying a cold ale with his friends would make him forget his problems. Why complicate his life when he could live like this forever?

****

Saturday brought showery weather and a strong southerly wind, a typical Wellington day. After clearing away the breakfast dishes, Alana packed a few clothes into Jason's car and they were soon driving towards the Hutt Valley and Jason's apartment. There was a rugby match at the local grounds in the afternoon and Jason needed to catch up on a few chores beforehand.

Alana hadn't watched rugby for a number of years, not since her brother Sandy had played in the junior grades back in Taupo. She dressed warmly and when they climbed up to sit in the crowded grandstand she looked around with interest. Many of the children had painted their faces with their team's colours and some wore colourful wigs. Music played over a loudspeaker and the atmosphere was alive with anticipation.

Cold cans of beer and containers of hot chips were in evidence and the crowd was in high spirits as the two teams streamed onto the field from the dressing sheds. Jason had located some of his mates in the crowd and was keen for them to meet Alana. This would have to wait until the end of the match, however, as the noise level was so loud that conversation was almost impossible.

Although Alana didn't really understand the rules, she soon got caught up in the excitement of the match in which the scores were even at half time. The home team surged ahead after the break and eventually took out the match much to the excitement of the crowd.

"Come on, we'll catch up with the guys in the clubrooms for a beer. Then we can see what everyone is up to tonight." Jason was happy to be on his home turf and hoped Alana was enjoying the day as well.

"Sure. We don't have any plans, so let's go with the flow," she agreed. They headed for the clubrooms and Jason made his way to the bar where he ordered two cans of lager and handed one to Alana. Soon they were standing around a high table with a dozen or so of his friends, who studied Alana with interest.

Jason explained how they had met and Carla, one of the girlfriends, welcomed her into their group. "It's good to see our friend with a nice partner," she said, and the others raised their glasses in response.

It seemed that there was to be a party in one of their flats later in the evening and Jason looked at Alana enquiringly to see whether she wanted to go along. She readily agreed as she was enjoying the company and so it was arranged. Luckily the flat was in walking distance to Jason's apartment so drinking and driving would not be an issue.

Alana knew that life back in Taupo would have been much like this. She realised that her life in Wellington was definitely a little dull. The other young women in the group were certainly very attractive but she felt at ease with them and she was looking forward to getting to know them better.

After a couple of beers they returned to Jason's apartment for a quick meal before gathering up some wine, beer and a bag of potato chips and walking the short distance to the party.

Pete and Sharon shared an old villa with another couple and the party was well underway by the time they arrived. They could hear the music as they walked up the driveway and several young people were sitting around on low couches and over-stuffed armchairs in the large lounge and hallway. They welcomed Jason and Alana who found a seat and poured themselves a drink.

Carla and her boyfriend Aaron came over and joined them, settling on the bright rug which covered the wooden floorboards. "I hope this rowdy bunch won't put you off. Jason is actually a quiet person as you probably know." Carla smiled up at Alana. She explained that she had just started a new job as an occupational therapist at the city hospital and had recently moved to the area from a small country town.

"It sounds as if we have a lot in common." Alana was pleased to have found a new friend. "I have a couple more papers to complete for my degree and then I guess I will be looking for a permanent job too."

"Maybe we could have a meal together next weekend. We could go to the tavern or the new Thai restaurant down the street. We can make up our minds closer to the time."

The next two hours passed quickly as Alana learned more about Jason's friends, then it was time to return to the apartment after a very eventful day.

Chapter 21

A whole week went by before John was in touch with Mary again. He had discussed the sale of the barber's shop with Nick who was happy to raise the funds needed to purchase the business. He would lease the premises from John Cameron who would continue to operate the bath house and weight training studio.

The day had started out fine and sunny but in the early afternoon a sudden heavy shower of rain took everybody by surprise. John was talking to the workers in the butcher's store two doors down the street and hurried back to the shelter of the salon. He climbed the steep staircase to his rooms above and took off his damp coat and hung it over the back of a chair.

He thought about writing a piece for the city paper and sat down with pen in hand. He had written some brief notes about a well attended funeral the day before. It wouldn't be too difficult to compose a story about the old gentleman who had died, but he felt restless and wandered over to the window to look out onto the dismal scene outside.

The sound of hoof beats on the cobbled street caught his attention. Whoever was outside was in for a wet ride. Next moment he was surprised to hear a shout from Nick and he poked his head out the door to see what was going on.

"You've got a visitor and a very wet one at that." Nick's voice came up from the lower level. Full of curiosity, John hurried down the staircase and could hardly believe his eyes to see the slender figure of Mary Gregg, her hat and coat sodden and her boots dripping with water.

She looked such a sorry sight that he guided her into the bath house where thick towels hung on wall racks. She gratefully accepted the towel and managed to discard the heavy coat and hat. "Let me help you take off your boots and then we will have a warm drink while your clothes dry."

Without hesitation, Mary followed John up the stairs and into the living area above.

"I must look like a drowned rat," she laughed. She attempted to dry her hair with the rough towel as John set a pot of water on the wood stove and spooned some tea into a china pot. A jar of sweet biscuits was produced and set on the crowded table.

"Welcome to my humble abode." John moved the clutter of papers aside and set cups and saucers and matching plates out on the table. Soon he had poured the boiling water into the tea pot and sat down waiting for the tea to draw.

"No-one predicted this heavy shower," Mary said. "My father and the other farmers will be glad of it after the dry spell but it certainly caught me by surprise."

"Then it is lucky for me to be able to share your company. How do you take your tea? A little milk and sugar, if I recall." John poured the tea into the cups and handed one to Mary with a sweeping gesture.

"This is certainly a nice surprise for me as well and a perfect excuse to see you. We enjoyed the entertainment at our home last week and I was wondering when I would see you again."

"I have been seriously considering my position and will sell the barber's business to young Nick. I now need to consider my options before seeking your parents' permission to court you. I couldn't expect you to live with me in these crowded rooms."

"A long engagement would be in order and there will be plenty of time to consider where we would live when the time comes." Mary smiled beguilingly in his direction. "I would certainly like to advance our friendship."

John was taken by surprise at Mary's boldness. Up until now she had been shy in his presence and now you could almost say she was being flirtatious. They sipped the hot tea and selected a biscuit from the jar.

Mary's hair had fallen down around her shoulders and the fine wool dress she wore clung to her slender figure. Her feet were bare as she had removed her damp stockings revealing slim ankles and small feet.

John caught his breath for a moment. His resolve had melted away. He desired this woman and she was right here in his room. He moved towards her and took her in his arms. She didn't resist as he picked her up and carried her into his bedroom and laid her on the bed.

He carefully unbuttoned her dress and slipped it off then her petticoat followed. He kissed her tenderly as he unfastened his shirt. Mary was lost in his caresses. She trembled as he kissed her neck, then uncovered her breast. His lips were playful until she felt her senses aroused. His mouth followed the contour of her body and she shuddered in his arms.

He pulled back. This was not the way to win her parents' approval. Then he stood up and fastened his shirt. "I'm sorry. I didn't mean to go this far."

Mary was flustered. She knew their lovemaking should stop but her body was urging her to go further. She threw her arms around his neck and pulled his hard body against her own. He hesitated for a moment and then responded to her embrace.

The fastenings on her skirt had parted and he clutched the long white petticoat and pulled it aside. She helped him by pulling open the bodice which bound her breasts and sighed as he kissed the buds until they responded. Little by little the layers of clothing were pealed away until she lay, her white skin glistening in the pale light.

Soon they lay together naked under a sheet as he let his fingers explore her body. He led her hand to grasp his arousal and guide it towards her. He was gentle at first and then exploded into the depths of her body as he climaxed. Then they lay together in a satisfied silence.

****

Alana and Jason's love making was getting more intense. Their bodies responded in unison and Jason was only just able to pull on a condom before they climaxed together. Once again Alana vowed to see a doctor the following week to get contraceptive advice. It was many months since she had been in a relationship and her prescription was out of date.

Sunday was spent resting and reading until it was time for Alana to return to the city and Jason to make the journey back to Springvale. He had an early start planned for Monday morning so would need to return that night.

"Why don't you come and join me later in the week? I'm sure you would like to revisit the Springvale museum and gather some more stories for your project. You could also visit your old friend John Cameron." Jason spoke in a teasing way and Alana agreed that there was more to discover about the milling history back in Springvale.

"Would Jan and Bruce mind us sharing a room? We have only known each other for such a short time." Alana felt a little awkward at returning to the tavern.

"They'd be delighted. Jan has been trying to get me married off for years." Jason laughed and ruffled her hair. "We'd better be off as heavy rain is forecast."

Back at her flat, Alana reluctantly said her goodbyes and ran up the short flight of steps to her door. Light rain had begun to fall and she switched on the light to brighten the room. She folded her laundry which had dried on the airing rack and searched in the refrigerator for something for dinner. They had eaten well all weekend so a quick snack was all that she needed.

She decided to phone her mother who was interested to hear of her new boyfriend. "You must bring this Jason to Taupo for a weekend. I would like to meet this fascinating young man." Her mother sounded happy that Alana was in a suitable relationship. "There is plenty of room for you to stay out on the farm."

Alana smiled. Her mother would love to see her but preferred not to clutter her perfect little townhouse with overnight visitors. Living in an old farmhouse had not been an ideal lifestyle for Margaret Cooper. She suspected that her mother might have a new male friend. She had mentioned a man named Frank several times, a widower whom she had met at the local bridge club. Maybe her mother was having a secret love affair as well.

Chapter 22

After their love making, Mary silently dressed, averting her eyes from John's masculine body. She couldn't believe her own boldness but apart from the sharp pain as John entered her, the sensations his touch aroused were new and exciting. She looked forward with anticipation to her birthday celebrations when she was certain that they would be betrothed.

John said little as he pulled on his trousers and shirt. He hadn't meant to go that far with this young woman but he had been celibate for too long and her willingness had urged him on.

"I'm sorry. That should not have happened. I hope you don't think too badly of me." He was apologetic as he retrieved Mary's coat from the bath house where it had been drying by the fire.

"I know I should never have encouraged you the way I did, but I have no regrets." Mary smiled up at him and he took her in his arms. "But now I had better ride back to the farm before the rain comes down again. I will pick up some fresh buns from the tea shop which will please my father I am sure."

John watched Mary ride away and then tried once again to put words on paper for the newspaper article. The old gentleman who had died was one of the early pioneers and he had written a diary containing many interesting anecdotes of life in the middle of the last century.

There was a time when he was ready to plough his new piece of land and no fewer than 20 of his neighbours turned out with an assortment of horses and ploughs to make the job easier. That was the spirit that had built the settlement of Clifton in those early days.

As well as building their own houses from trees milled on the land, the pioneering families joined together to build churches and a school, providing much needed centres to meet and socialise.

The story was soon taking shape and John realised that he could be spending more time on his writing. It would compensate for the lack of earnings from the bath house. Soon he had finished and signed his name with a flourish. The rain had stopped so he wasted no time in taking the envelope to the store where the post was sorted. Hopefully, the story would appear in the city paper during the next week.

****

Back at the tavern in Springvale Jason had an early start to meet the roading contractors out on the job. They were planning to divert the country road to avoid a sharp bend which had been the scene of several motor vehicle accidents.

Soon they were checking the details on a large map and Jason knew that this job could take another few weeks. He had hoped to be finished at Springvale by the end of the following week, but this new project could delay him from returning to Wellington.

"It looks as though I'll be staying here for longer than I thought," he said, when he returned to the tavern later that afternoon.

"We don't mind how long you stay. And you really must invite Alana to join you whenever she can. We wouldn't charge any extra for the room so she would only pay for meals." Bruce was anxious to retain such a good, steady guest.

"I'm not sure where Alana's next job will take her, but I'm hoping that she will join me here later in the week." Jason was already missing his new friend and was looking forward to her company in a few days' time. Once she started her next project there was no knowing where she would be based.

With any luck she would find something close to the city so they could spend their weekends together. They could even spend a few days in Taupo before he started the roading project. With this in mind, Jason took out his phone and texted Alana's number. "You are welcome to stay here any time. Look forward to seeing you. Love, Jason."

The reply came a few moments later. "I'll be there Wed. Love you too, Alana." This brought a smile to Jason's face as he joined Bruce Evans for a beer at the bar. The young farmers' group was due in for a meal soon and Jason knew there would be plenty of company tonight.

With just a week to go before the museum project was due to be completed, Alana was anxious to receive the death certificate for John Cameron. She phoned the maritime museum and sure enough, they had received the document so she wasted no time pulling on a warm coat and walking briskly along the waterfront. It was about a 20-minute stroll past the fishing boats docked at the pier and the old wharf buildings.

Estelle Jones greeted her when she arrived and handed her the document which would hopefully answer a few questions. The name and date of death was recorded and the parents were Donald Cameron and Margaret Stirling,

Donald born in Argyle and Margaret in Ayrshire, Scotland. Married state was unknown. Cause of death, pneumonia, following exposure. A street address was given in the settlement of Springvale.

"I know from the newspaper article that John was engaged to Mary Gregg at her 18th birthday party. Perhaps they didn't marry and it doesn't mention any children." Alana had found a few more answers but was disappointed that a spouse wasn't mentioned.

"He may have gone to the mill to earn the money before they could be married. It happened quite frequently in those difficult times," said Estelle. "You could return to Springvale and finish your research there. We will pay for a few more days at the tavern."

Alana was excited that she could go back to Springvale with the blessing of the museum committee. She would have her own room and was sure that there was more to discover back in the small village and it would be great to be reunited with Jason.

****

Mary was so busy planning her 18th birthday party that she could think of little else, although every time she thought about the wet afternoon at John's dwelling a shiver of excitement ran through her. She wanted to look her best for such an important occasion and her mother had promised her a new gown to be made by the dressmaker in town. Her hair would be dressed in a formal style and she would carry a small fan and a beaded purse which her mother had brought over from their home in England.

Elias Gregg was also busy with the arrangements for his daughter's birthday party. He consulted his wife several times. "Should we hold it in the school or the hall in Clifton?"

"Why not decorate the barn. It would be more convenient to hold the party on our property," was her advice. And so it was decided. Bales of hay would be placed around the barn for seating and long trestle tables set up for the food.

The young people spent many hours making wreaths and streamers from coloured paper to decorate the walls, and lanterns would provide the lighting. A piano could be moved into the barn and the schoolmaster's wife would provide the music for the dancing.

Beer and punch could be provided along with lemonade for the ladies. Food was sure to be plentiful with several of the neighbours offering to bring along their favourite dishes. Mary's mother was already busy preparing jars of fruit and pickles, and loaves of bread and slabs of cake would be baked nearer the time.

Elias Gregg planned to supply a pig and a hogget which would be cooked slowly on a spit over a fire. Vegetables of all descriptions would be roasted in the embers and jugs of custard served with the bowls of fruit. Plates of hard-boiled eggs on beds of lettuce and slices of crusty bread as well as slices of cold ham and pickled onions would adorn the decorated tables.

Mary's sister and brother were envious at all the fuss. "It's just another birthday," they moaned. "We will do the same when you reach the age of 18. It's a very special occasion and we want to celebrate it in style," their parents assured them.

Mary was anxious that John had not arranged a meeting with her parents to ask for their consent to an engagement. She was hoping for a pretty ring to show off at the party.

She took the opportunity to call into the salon when she visited the town with her parents. He didn't invite her upstairs this time, but instead they met rather formally on the porch outside the building. "Would you like to come to tea some time this week? I'm sure you would like a conversation with my family." Mary felt a little nervous as she hadn't spoken to John since their romantic encounter.

"I would be pleased to be there, my dear. I am most anxious for your parents to think well of me." John felt that everything was moving too fast for his liking. He knew that Mary was expecting to announce their engagement at the birthday party, but his financial situation was on shaky ground.

He softened when he saw the look of pleasure that came over her face. She was certainly a very attractive young woman and had already shown a desire to please his every need.

"I'll join you for tea next Wednesday and will take the opportunity to talk to your parents." She gave him a quick hug and then went out onto the street to join the family.

Chapter 23

Wednesday morning dawned fine and clear and Alana wasted no time in packing her bag and setting off in the direction of Springvale. She knew that Jason would be working and she probably wouldn't see him until night-fall, but she wanted to spend more time at the museum to read through the old records.

She called at the tavern and took her gear up to her al-lotted room. Jan Cameron smiled as she directed Alana to a room right beside Jason's. She knew they would probably get together as the evening wore on and was happy that the two of them seemed so contented.

"It's a match made in heaven," she whispered to her husband who was tidying the bar for the lunch time crowd. He smiled at her enthusiasm. "Yes, those two certainly seem to be getting along okay. You might say you have succeeded in playing Cupid once again."

Jan laughed. There was nothing she liked better than a fine romance and it didn't happen too often in their little country tavern. But now there was lunch to prepare and she headed for the kitchen.

There were several guests booked in for tonight and an unknown number of casual diners to be catered for. It was a busy life but she enjoyed every moment of it.

Alana packed away her belongings and headed down the street towards the village. She knew the address of the house where John Cameron had lived and she was anxious to locate it. It didn't take too long to find the street and a row of old houses greeted her. Number 32 Grange Street proved to be a 19th century villa which had been extensively renovated and she photographed it as she walked by. That was John Cameron's last address and she would love to find out who had owned it back in the timber milling days.

Back at the museum she found an old phone directory and leafed through the pages. Few homes were listed as many had not joined the local telephone exchange. There was no listing for number 32 Grange Street.

"Where else could I find any information about this house?" she asked and Flo Avery located an old trade directory for the area. "There could be something here." She handed Alana the tattered book.

Sure enough, 32 Grange Street was listed as a boarding house, run by Mrs Emily Todd. "Home comforts and wholesome meals at reasonable rates," the advertisement read.

Alana was interested to learn that John Cameron had moved from the small cabin at the mill site into more comfortable living quarters. The rest of the directory made interesting reading as it painted a picture of the town as it was back in the timber milling days.

Three hotels were listed including the Imperial, which she knew was the original name for the Springvale Tavern. There were at least 10 other stores all clustered together in the centre of the village. A coach builder and wheelwright, blacksmith, livery and stables, billiard saloon and barber's shop were also listed, all advertising their services. This information would certainly add colour to the story of John Cameron.

It didn't take long to scan the pages and send them to her email and then Alana walked back to the cemetery to revisit the unmarked grave. She placed a rose from the garden in a glass jar which was lying on the grass and said a silent prayer to the man buried under the turf. She knew more about him than she had a few short weeks ago but there were still secrets to be unveiled.

****

Mary was looking forward to John Cameron's visit on Wednesday but was afraid to broach the subject of a possible engagement to her parents. She knew that they liked the man, but were doubtful about his future. However, he did come from a well respected family in the district who would be among the guests at Mary's birthday party.

"He seems to have too many strings to his bow. If he were to stick to journalism or run the barber's shop, that would provide an adequate income, but he seems to move from one thing to another." Mary's mother was anxious to do the right thing for her eldest daughter.

"I think Mr Cameron is a bit of an adventurer. He had a good education in the city, dabbled in journalism, then got involved in this fitness and weight training which is almost an obsession," Elias Gregg agreed. "But our Mary seems to have her sights set on the man and I don't see too much harm coming from allowing an engagement."

Mary sighed. Her daughter seemed much too young to be betrothed, but then she was not much older when she married Elias all those years ago. She took her husband's hand. "If they are as fortunate as you and I we will be truly blessed," she said.

When the big day came Mary finished her chores early and helped her mother prepare the evening meal. John arrived promptly at six o'clock and was invited into the living room where a bottle of sherry was produced. The

Greggs might be church-going people, but they enjoyed a celebratory drink when the occasion arose.

Jean and William were hanging about, wanting to hear the conversation but were sent away, leaving John and Mary alone with her parents. Mary sat primly, with her hands folded in her lap. John, on the other hand, appeared relaxed and confident and was soon enthralling the Greggs with his humorous accounts of reporting at meetings and trying to stay awake when the speeches became too ponderous.

When young Mary was sent from the room to check the dinner which was cooking on the stove, Elias broached the subject they had come together to discuss. "I believe you have plans to marry our daughter," he said, without preamble. "We feel she is too young for marriage but would not object to an engagement of some length."

John stood and shook Elias' hand with a firm grip. "It would be an honour to be engaged to your delightful daughter," he said. "I would try to give her a good life."

"Then let us call the young lady in and see what she has to say." Elias stood and opened the door, beckoning Mary to come back into the living room.

"Your mother and I have agreed to your betrothal to Mr John Cameron if that is what you desire." Mary flew into her mother's arms and then gave her father a quick peck on the cheek. Her face was flushed with excitement as she stood beside her suitor who took her hand and sat her down beside him on the over-stuffed sofa.

"Oh yes. I would be most happy to be with John for the rest of my days," she said in a trembling voice. "I would try to please him in every way." Then Mary was handed a small glass of the sweet sherry which she sipped delicately.

"You can come in now and congratulate your sister. She and John are engaged to be married and have our blessing." Elias opened the door to the younger members of the family who were offered a small glass of the sweet liquid as a special treat.

"Well, I believe it is time to eat the meal before it spoils." Mary's mother was soon busy in the kitchen dishing the food into large bowls and placing them on the table which had been set with the best silver cutlery. Starched linen napkins had been placed beside each setting and soon they were all sitting around the table passing the food from one to the other, and enjoying the festive atmosphere.

Chapter 24

The afternoon passed quickly as Alana worked on her notes and added the information about Springvale in the town's hey day. She could see the row of shops from her window and it was easy to imagine the way they would have looked back in the time of John Cameron. Most of the verandahs had not been altered but the facades had recently been painted in bright colours.

She had noticed a retirement home along the street from the old boarding house and decided that she would call there the next day and talk to some of the residents. There were sure to be several in their 90s who might remember the way it was. With any luck, some may even have worked at the timber mill.

She was still looking out of the window when Jason's utility pulled into the driveway and parked behind the tavern. She restrained herself from rushing down the stairs to greet him but hurriedly combed her hair and daubed on some lip gloss.

She heard him come up the stairs and open his door and then a few moments later there was a gentle tap on her door and Jason was there, a smile on his face, his arms outstretched in greeting.

"I really missed you," they both began speaking together and next thing Jason was inside the room and they were in each other's arms. "Just give me time to shower and change and we can go down and celebrate with a drink."

Alana packed her assignment away and changed into a tidy blouse. It felt so good to be back with Jason. She had really missed his company while he was gone. Ten minutes later they were on their way down the stairs. "Here come the love birds," Bruce called out from behind the bar. "Sit yourselves down and we'll celebrate Alana's return in style.

They laughed as they chose two stools and waited for Bruce to bring the drinks. He had poured a pint of ale for himself and raised his glass in their direction. "We've missed you, lassie," he said. "We got used to seeing your smiling face.'

"I've missed you all as well," Alana answered. "Life seems very dull back in the big city after all the excitement of Springvale."

Bruce laughed at the thought that researching a cemetery could be considered more exciting than the pace of life in Wellington. "Ah well, everything depends on the company that you're keeping."

Alana smiled at Jason and nodded in agreement. "Yes, it was certainly the good company that was missing."

Jan came into the room and gave them both a hug. "Good to have you back," she said. "There is quite a crowd coming in tonight so if you want dinner here it might pay to book in before the rush."

Neither Alana nor Jason were ready to eat so early so they took their drinks over to the comfortable couch in front of a gas fire as the evening was getting a little chilly.

"How has your week been?" Alana asked. Jason explained about the new roading project which would keep him in Springvale for a few more weeks. "At least you can come and join me here and we will have weekends together," he said.

Alana hadn't given much thought to her future plans but hoped that she would find some work close by. She

152

would have to start making enquiries soon as she needed the income to pay for her apartment.

But tonight was not the time to worry about details. She and Jason were back together and ready to enjoy a great night among old friends.

****

With the birthday party just days away, John Cameron visited the Gregg household a number of times to help with the preparations. He and Mary worked together as they decorated the barn and helped set up the tables. Several of William's friends were given the task of bringing in the hay bales which were stored in a lean-to attached to the barn.

Several hay fights were threatened but a stern look from Elias kept the lads in order. No-one wanted the job of cleaning up after a hay fight. Jean and Mary would arrange vases of flowers closer to the day of the party and the task of moving the heavy piano had been left to a number of willing farm hands.

"Everything is looking very grand," said John as he stood back and looked around the decorated barn, now festooned with streamers and paper bows. "I'm sure the district will be talking about this party for months to come."

"I know they are in for a big surprise when our engagement is announced. Many of the young women will be very envious, I am sure." Mary still couldn't believe that she and this handsome man were about to be betrothed.

They had collected her new gown from the dressmaker and she was thrilled with the result. Dark green brocade had been chosen, nipped in at the waist with a wide skirt and small pearl buttons down the front. The neckline was becomingly low and she blushed when she looked in the mirror and observed the swell of her bosom above the cream lace edging.

The day before the party Mary visited the barber's salon and John took the opportunity to steer her in the direction of the tiny jewellery store where they selected a dainty ring with one small diamond. "I plan to buy you a larger ring one day, but accept this with my love," John said as he placed the ring on her finger. Mary studied it for a moment and then it was packed away in its box until after the engagement had been announced.

Soon the carriage was filled with last minute items needed for the celebrations. Kegs of beer had been lifted into place and bags of sugar and flour piled high.

John watched as they set off through the town, waving to the townspeople as they drove by. In a few hours he would be an engaged man. What would the future hold for him and Mary?

****

In spite of her good intentions, Alana urged Jason to spend the night in her room and when they woke next morning he gathered up his clothing and returned stealthily to his own room to dress ready for the day's work. He had already finished breakfast by the time Alana appeared, and set off in the utility to return to the old saw mill site.

Tonight they planned to eat at the restaurant across the street and Alana had a full day to go through the records at the museum and visit the retirement home. Although she knew that they could easily have shared a room, while the museum grant was paying for her accommodation she may as well take advantage of the extra space.

Flo Avery had found more information about the boarding house in Grange Street. There were several advertisements in the local papers at the time and a short account of the sale of the property to Mrs Emily Todd. It seems that she had moved from the South Island to run the boarding house. Perhaps she had descendents who might have more information.

"Stanley Todd owns the local garage. Perhaps he is a relative. It might be worth asking him. He's been around the area for ever and his father before him." Flo was beginning to take a keen interest in Alana's research.

"That sounds like a great idea. I'll go along and see if he is available right now." Alana picked up the information about Mrs Todd and the boarding house and headed a few doors along the road to the busy repair shop. There were several cars and trucks parked outside and a couple of grease stained mechanics working on a variety of vehicles.

A middle-aged man in a faded overall greeted her at the door. "And how can I help you, young lady?" he queried.

"I'm looking for information about a Mrs Emily Todd who owned a boarding house many years ago. Is the name familiar to you?"

"You just happen to be asking about my great grandmother who ran an establishment in Grange Street. A real old character she was. Come into the lunch room and tell me what you want to know. By the way, the name's Stan."

The lunch room was as cluttered as the rest of the garage, and Stan wiped off a chair and pulled it up to the dilapidated table. Alana laid the papers down on the table and explained the purpose of the visit. "Do you know whether Mrs Todd kept records of her guests and whether they would still be available?"

"I'm not sure what records we have but I know we cleared a lot of boxes of papers from my old man's garage when we moved him into the home. I always meant to go through them and find out what's there but never got around to it."

Alana felt a tingle of excitement. She may have stumbled upon a mine of information here. "Would you mind if I take a look? I'm really keen to learn more about the boarding house and its occupants."

"No worries. The boxes are over in the corner and we can move them into the lunch room. It would be good to find out what is there."

Stan strolled over to a stack of boxes, picked up the first two and placed them on the lunch table. "Go for it. No-one has looked through those boxes for years. Now I'm curious to know what is inside."

Alana gingerly opened the first box. The contents smelt musty and she picked up the first bundle of documents. They turned out to be accounts and receipts from a later era. This was not what she was after. The second box yielded a number of rates demands and mortgage repayments. She needed to find something from an earlier time.

She carried the two boxes back and pulled out one right at the bottom of the pile. Perhaps this would contain something more interesting. Indeed, she pulled out a hard covered book with names and columns of figures.

She realised that it was a list of tenants and their payments.

She opened the faded pages carefully. The first date was January 1906 when there were six men listed in the dwelling. By the time she came to 1912, there were 10 names in the book. Would she find the elusive John Cameron? She had almost lost hope when there it was, the name she was hoping to find.

John Cameron was renting room number five, with use of the bathroom and two meals a day provided. It appeared that he paid faithfully every week for about six months but then his name disappeared from the records on 30 August 1912.

Alana took the book to Stan and asked permission to photocopy the relevant pages. Perhaps there were other notes in the boxes. Maybe a diary or note book of some sort. She pulled a battered journal from the bottom of the box. It seemed that Emily Todd had made a few random notes describing some of her tenants. She described several of the men as hard and uncouth. She spoke of some as being sad and lonely, away from their wives and families. She worried that several of them worked too hard, then squandered their hard-earned wages at the taverns.

Alana knew that these historic papers should be in safe keeping at the museum. She would tell Flo Avery about her find and let her persuade Stan to hand over the documents. There was much more reading to be done here, but now she wanted to visit the retirement home and meet some of the residents.

Stan Todd was sorry to see her go. "Come back any time and look through more of the boxes." When she told him where she was heading he told her to ask for Norman Todd, his father, who enjoyed a friendly chat.

"My old man will be able to tell you more about our Emily," he laughed.

Chapter 25

Almost everyone in the small district of Clifton had received an invitation to Mary Gregg's 18th birthday party. John and his family had been invited to share a light meal before the event and they received the news of the intended engagement with some surprise.

"I am so happy for you, my dear," Margaret Cameron gave Mary a hug when she heard the news. But secretly she was not so sure. How was her son going to afford to set up a home for this young woman? "Congratulations. It's certainly time you found yourself a wife." She gave her son a hug and looked at young Mary with interest.

Last time she had set eyes on her was in the classroom as she received a prize that Donald had donated.

Horses and carriages were beginning to arrive and the guests were escorted into the barn by young William and his friends. Mary was nervous as she dressed in her new finery. Would she be over dressed for the occasion? Most of the women were wearing warm clothing suitable for the outdoors, though several of the younger set had thrown warm coats over their light dresses.

John looked elegant in his black jacket and grey waistcoat. He took Mary by the hand and led her into the crowded barn. "You look very beautiful, my dear. Come and meet your guests and enjoy your special night."

Mary took a deep breath and allowed herself to be led into the midst of the revelers who were already relaxing with a glass of beverage. She took a small tumbler of punch from her father and moved among the guests thanking them for their attendance.

It had been decided to serve dinner early in the evening and several of the women were clustered in the kitchen of the house completing the last minute preparations. Elias was busy carving the meat from the spit and the vegetables were lifted onto heated trays. The cold meats and salad had been set around the tables and jugs of gravy were warming on the stove.

Soon everyone was called to sit at the tables and the minister from the church said grace. The hot meat and vegetables were spooned onto the plates and handed to the seated guests who helped themselves to the other delicacies from the assortment on the tables.

There was a buzz of conversation as the food was consumed. Then small plates of fruit were handed out and jugs of creamy custard passed around. As the meal was nearing completion, Elias stood up and banged his spoon on the table to get everybody's attention.

"We are here tonight to celebrate the coming of age of our elder daughter Mary. It also gives her mother and myself great pleasure in announcing her engagement to John Cameron. I ask you to raise your glasses and drink a toast to the happy couple."

John touched a glass of sherry onto Mary's glass and they looked at each other as they took a mouthful of the rich beverage. Then several of the guests crowded around offering their congratulations and admiring the ring which John had placed on Mary's finger.

It didn't take long to clear the tables and drag them back against the wall of the barn. The school master's wife sat at the piano and began pounding the keys, a signal for the dancing to begin. Elias claimed the first dance with his daughter and John took her mother by the arm and led her onto the floor for a sedate waltz. Soon everyone was on their feet and the floor of the barn was vibrating from the movement.

"I think the evening is going exceptionally well," Mrs Gregg said as John spun her around in an intricate twirl.

"There's no doubt about it. This will be the event of the year in Clifton," John replied. They returned to their seats and a foxtrot was announced. This time John took Mary in his arms and whirled her onto the floor. "Now it's our turn, my lovely. We will give them something to talk about."

They spun around in time to the music until Mary felt quite dizzy. She closed her eyes and relaxed in John's arms. She was so happy that she wanted this night to go on for ever.

****

Alana reluctantly dragged herself away from the old garage and called at the lunch bar to buy a sandwich. She could eat that and then call at the retirement home to talk to Stan Todd's father. She made enquiries at the front desk and was shown into a large lounge where several elderly people were sitting in armchairs, most of them asleep.

The duty nurse led her over to Norman Todd and gently shook him by the shoulder. "You've got a lady visitor, Norm. You wouldn't want to miss out on that." The man opened his eyes and blinked at Alana. Then he sat upright in his chair and leaned in her direction.

"You're certainly a sight for sore eyes, my dear. Why is a pretty young thing like you visiting all the geriatrics?" He threw his head back and laughed. "Pull a chair up beside me. My hearing's not what it used to be."

Alana explained that she had been talking to his son and was interested in the old boarding house run by Stan's great grandmother.

Norm sat up even straighter. "That place was my grandmother's life," he said. "She treated those men like her own sons. Anybody who stayed in Emily Todd's boarding house was very lucky indeed."

"Were they mostly single men or did some of them have wives and families back in their home towns?" Alana was curious to learn all she could.

"Most were single and saving to marry their sweethearts back home. Others were forced to leave their families to find work where the money was good. Times were bad back then." Norm Todd leaned back in his chair and clasped his hands together. "It was the war that saved the country. Once the Great War started everyone wanted all the produce we could spare to feed the troops."

"Has the house in Grange Street changed very much since your grandmother's days? It must be a large property as she had 10 lodgers at one stage."

"There were a lot of small rooms, not much more than lean-tos when she had the boarding house. Some of those were pulled down and several of the rooms have recently been enlarged they tell me."

"Do you mind me looking through the papers that are stored at the garage? Your son tells me they came from your home when you moved out." Alana knew there would be more information to be gleaned from the old storage boxes.

"Help yourself lass. They are only memories for an old codger like me. You are welcome to them." Norman began to grow weary and Alana knew that it was time to leave. She would call again another day.

Alana realised she was letting the mysterious John Cameron take over her life. Even in the night her dreams were filled with John Cameron. She kept visualising the lonely, unmarked grave and imagining a lonely ghost standing in the graveyard. She needed to focus on completing her assignment and then move on.

She walked back through the town and couldn't resist going past the old boarding house one more time. Back at the tavern she leafed through the pile of notes and set them in order. Soon she was busy transferring the information onto her laptop. The story of old Springvale was beginning to emerge.

****

The days following the 18th birthday party and his engagement to Mary Gregg were anxious ones for John Cameron. Buying the engagement ring for Mary had made a big hole in his bank account and used up much of the money that Nick had paid for the barber shop business.

With the down turn in the economy, the bath house was attracting very few customers and fewer young men could afford to attend his weight lifting lessons. Something would have to be done.

He was discussing the situation with his friend Joe in the butcher's shop when Joe pointed out an advertisement in a national newspaper. "If you really want to make big money in a hurry, maybe you should look at this," he said. John took the newspaper and read with interest about the opportunities in the timber settlement of Springvale.

"Mill hands and forestry workers urgently required. Accommodation provided, good wages for the right men. Only strong men need apply." He flexed his muscles and laughed.

"I don't think I would have too much trouble there, but Springvale is a long way from here. Right across the water in the North Island. I'm sure that young Mary would not like to see me go so far away."

"If you could work for a few months and earn enough to keep a roof over your heads, she may not object." Joe could see the possibilities and in fact, was considering taking up a position there himself.

John thoughtfully wrote down the contact details and returned to his rooms. There would be no harm done in making enquiries. After all, his parents had travelled many miles across the sea for a better future.

Chapter 26

Jason and Alana strolled along the quiet street later that day, heading for the western style restaurant. They were greeted by a waitress wearing a red checked apron and shown to a table in the corner. The juke box was already playing a slow country and western number.

"This is a nice change of pace," said Alana as they settled into their seats and studied the beverage list. There was a younger crowd patronising the restaurant, many of them ordering pizzas or hamburgers, then going on their way.

"I think I'd like to try a pizza. Would that be okay with you?"

Alana agreed and they selected two pizzas from the list and sat, enjoying their drinks and taking in the atmosphere.

"I'll be starting the roading project soon," Jason said. "But I could probably take a few days off before that starts. Would you like to go away somewhere and have a break? When will your project be finished?"

Alana knew she had about a week's work left, depending on how much more time she spent on John Cameron's story. "Sounds great. I should be free about the same time and we could call at Taupo if you want. There's always plenty to do there and my mother would love to meet you."

Jason smiled. He had hoped to have a quiet time with Alana and staying with her family was not quite what he had in mind. "I'd like to travel around a bit. We could certainly spend a couple of nights in Taupo then maybe drive over to Napier."

"I'd love to do that. It's ages since I went to Napier and it's a beautiful place to visit." Alana was excited at the prospect of taking a break. "We could spend a night at the farm and take in the sites of Taupo then enjoy the orchards and wine country as well as the art nouveau buildings in Napier."

They agreed not to make bookings as it was outside the holiday season and they knew accommodation would be plentiful. The pizzas arrived and the evening continued pleasantly. After they had eaten, they strolled down to the park and river before heading back to the tavern where they took a cup of coffee up to Jason's room and watched television.

Alana returned to her own room that night as Jason had an early start and there was no reason for her to get up early. Now that she was on a tight deadline she wanted to complete her assignment as soon as possible and would work into the night.

****

As soon as John Cameron returned to his quarters he sat down and wrote a letter of application to the address in the advertisement. He would wait to hear back before broaching the subject with Mary. He had been invited to the farm the next evening for a meal but wouldn't mention the possibility of work in Springvale.

He had seen Mary only once since their engagement and he was careful not to commit himself to any plans for their future. He knew that she would like them to wed as soon as possible but did not want to fill her with false promises of an early wedding.

He realised that work in a timber mill would be hard, but his fitness training should pay off and it should not be a problem. He knew nothing of the town of Springvale which was a short distance from the capital city of Wellington where he would disembark if he went by steamer from Dunedin.

He would need to buy some sturdy boots and warm clothing for working in the forest or the mill. He may even have to supply his own axe and other equipment, but he would find out all the details if his application was successful.

He arrived at the Gregg's farm in a cheerful mood. Mary was happy to see him and they walked together in the garden before enjoying a drink in the summer house.

"You seem to be in a happy frame of mind." Mary was pleased to see John in such a relaxed state. She knew he had been worried about their future and wondered what had happened to change his attitude.

"I'm just glad to be with you and know that one day we will be married," he said.

"Come and sit beside me and tell me that you love me." He drew Mary into his arms, but she hesitated, afraid someone might interrupt them.

"My parents could come out at any time," she said. "We must find somewhere to meet where we can be alone."

"That is true. Another picnic by the river could be arranged or I could accompany you to the dance at the hall on Saturday night. Would your father loan us the horse and gig do you think?"

"I don't see why not. We must ask his permission, but I know that my sister Jean would want to come along." Mary knew it would be difficult to go out at night without a chaperone and Jean or William would probably be asked to accompany them.

At that moment, William appeared to say that the meal was ready. He seemed disappointed that he didn't catch them embracing. He knew his sister would have been so embarrassed.

As Elias carved the roast beef and Mary passed around the plates of vegetables, there was plenty of chatter. William was anxious to continue his fitness classes, but his father said he would have to earn the money to pay for the lessons.

Jean was hoping to be taken on officially as a student teacher the following term, for which she would be paid a small wage. Mary was quiet. Although she would love to find a paying job, it would mean living in Dunedin and she was loathe to move so far away from her fiancé.

John said little about his prospects. If he moved to Springvale to work in the timber mill there would be no reason for Mary to remain in Clifton. She had already been offered employment in her aunt's drapery store and she would be able to save towards their marriage. It could be the answer to all their problems.

****

Friday came around quickly for Alana as she worked through her notes and compiled the information ready to complete her project. Later in the day she and Jason would drive back to Wellington where they would spend the night at her apartment.

She decided that she had time to take another look through the boxes of papers and documents at Stan Todd's garage. She was keen to look more closely at the notes written by Emily Todd, describing several of her boarders.

With any luck there might be a reference to John Cameron and some clue as to how he had died. The fact that there were only a few short months separating the account of his engagement to the date of his death puzzled Alana and she wanted to find out more.

Stan greeted her warmly and carried a couple of the larger boxes into the lunch room. "My old man said that you had visited him. He was quite chuffed about it. I hope he was able to help you."

"It was great to meet your father. He was full of information and I'd love to talk to him again some time." Alana opened the first box and shook the dust from the pile of papers inside. Most of these were bills and receipts but a hard covered book at the bottom of the box caught her attention. She pulled out the book and opened the pages which were covered with hand written notes. There were lists of names and addresses as well as personal notes and Alana realised it was probably a registration book to help Emily Todd keep track of the boarders.

The boarding house had been operating for several years and Alana flicked through until she came to 1912. There in the middle of the page was the name she was looking for. "John Cameron, previously Main Street, Clifton. Requires two meals a day and cut lunch. Been staying at camp, has not been well with cough. Nice gentleman."

So John Cameron had started out in one of the rough huts at the mill site and moved to more comfortable accommodation. She scanned through the pages until she came across another entry. "John Cameron sends money to a lass called Mary. He says they hope to marry soon. His cough has improved. Enjoys my cooking!"

A few pages over and another reference. "John Cameron, popular at hotel, likes to sing songs of Scotland. He is anxious to marry soon."

Alana felt elated. She had stumbled on a gold mine, but she came to the end of the book without finding any further notes of interest. She glanced at the watch and realised it was time to return to the tavern and drive back to the city.

"Thanks so much. If you don't mind, I'll try to get back later next week and read some more of the documents." Alana said her goodbyes to Stan Todd and hurried back to her room where she gathered up all her papers and stowed them into a brief case. Then she looked around and located her clothing and other belongings and piled them into a bag.

Jan and Bruce Evans came out to see her off. "You must come back any time. We would love to see you," Jan said.

"I could be back next week, then Jason and I are hoping to take a short trip to Taupo and Napier before he starts his next project." Alana gave them a hug and was soon driving back towards the main road and the busy Friday afternoon traffic.

****

It took 10 days for John Cameron to receive a reply from the timber company. They urgently needed more workers and were willing to pay his steamer fare to Wellington. All equipment would be supplied but they advised warm clothing and sturdy boots.

Now John knew that he had to come to a decision. Working at the timber mill would sort out his financial problems, but what would Mary say when she found out about his plans?

He took the letter to the butcher's shop to share the news with his friend. "What do you think I should do? Mary wants to wed as soon as possible but I am in no position to offer her a future unless I take up this offer."

"You really have no choice," said Joe. "I would like to follow you but have a wife and family to consider."

John knew that this move to Springvale would be the answer to all his problems. Six months of hard work should bring sufficient reward to establish a home for Mary. He packed some food into a bag and set off on his horse to the Gregg farm. Mary was not expecting him but he knew that she would be pleased to accompany him down to the river where they had last spent time together.

When he arrived at the farm Mary was helping her mother with the laundry. The clothes had been washed and were being hung on the line to dry. "Please let me go, mother. I'll finish all the chores when I return," she pleaded.

Her mother smiled. She felt that Mary was in good hands and added some cool apple cider to the picnic bag. "Be off with you and enjoy the day," she said, as John and Mary rode off into the countryside in the direction of the river.

They reached the river bank and tethered their horses. John spread a rug over the grass and sat down, urging Mary to join him. She sat beside him, glancing at him shyly.

"Come on, my love. No-one can disturb us here." John took Mary in his arms and stroked her hair.

Mary relaxed and laid her head on his shoulder. A tremor of excitement ran through her body as John loosened her jacket and drew it over her shoulders. She turned to kiss him and he laid her gently onto the rug.

John kissed her deeply and removed his jacket. His shirt soon followed and Mary unfastened the buttons on her blouse. His mouth trailed down to her breasts which stood out under the fine fabric of her vest. They responded to his touch and he drew her closer, cradling her against his hard body.

They rolled over and Mary was on top of him, her hands fumbling with his shirt, which came away at her touch. Her hand ran through the thick hair on his chest and down over his taut stomach.

John unfastened the buttons on his trousers and her hand found its way downwards, her desire increasing as she felt his hardness.

"Are you sure about this, my Mary?" he gasped as his feelings threatened to take over.

Her answer was a passionate kiss as she rolled onto the rug and pulled her skirt aside revealing white linen undergarments fringed with lace. With a tug these were pulled away and her pale skin was revealed, tempting him to go further.

"I want you, my John," she whispered as she pulled him towards her and held him tantalisingly close. His fingers felt her wetness as he tenderly massaged her until she was moaning with desire, then he gently lowered himself until they were joined and her body responded to his thrusts.

Afterwards they lay together, the sounds of the water and the rustle of the leaves filling the silence. John's arms tightened around her as he thought of the news he would soon be sharing with her. He was loathe to break the spell that their love making had created, but the decision to work in Springvale still had to be made.

Chapter 27

Alana arrived back at the hillside apartment in the late afternoon and parked her car in the small garage behind the building. It took two trips to carry all her gear inside and she pulled open the curtains to let the sunlight into the room.

Jason would be arriving shortly and she needed to clear everything off the bed and put away the laundry she had left drying on the clothes rack. She searched in the freezer and pulled out two steaks which would go with the salad ingredients she had picked up from the supermarket on the way home.

They had planned to call at the boat house after the meal and catch up with some of Jason's friends and Alana was looking forward to meeting them again.

It wasn't long before Jason pulled into the parking space behind the apartment and Alana met him at the top of the steps. He carried a back pack and a bottle of wine which he handed to her with a smile. "I missed you at breakfast, but I needed to get away early. It's been quite a day meeting the new contractors and going over the roading plans."

Alana was about to tell him about her latest news of John Cameron, but hesitated. She knew that Jason thought she was becoming obsessed with Mr Cameron. Instead she asked him about the proposed trip to Taupo and pulled out a map of the North Island so they could plan their journey.

"I should have the project handed in next week and then I could come and spend some time with you at Springvale. I'd like to give a copy of my work to Flo

Avery at the museum." Alana was excited that the work was almost completed and they were taking an unexpected holiday.

"Sounds good. You can share my room at the tavern any time. I really miss you when you're not around."

While Alana prepared the salad, Jason fired up the gas barbecue on the back porch and soon the meal was ready, and served up on the round table in front of the window overlooking the sea. The rowers were out in force and small yachts came into view every so often.

"You really do have a nice outlook. Much better than the back yard at my place," Jason said.

"Yes, but your unit is much larger than this tiny place. It would be very crowded if two people lived here."

"I think it's cosy. I know I wouldn't mind." Jason gave Alana and hug and she found herself blushing. She was beginning to think that they might move in together at some stage, but they still had a lot to learn about each other.

"At the moment I feel like a gipsy, living at three addresses. But I guess that's the nature of our lifestyle. I will have to look for my next job soon. Goodness only knows where I might end up." Alana began clearing the dishes away and went into the bathroom to renew her make up.

It was around seven o'clock when they headed for the boat house where the rugby crowd would be gathered to watch the game.

****

After their memorable picnic beside the river, Mary could hardly wait for Saturday night when John was to drive the horse and cart to the dance at the local hall. Both Jean and William were coming along as well and Jean hoped to catch up with Nick Postles.

John arrived early and was greeted by Elias who gave instructions on how the horse should be handled. They were all dressed in warm coats to keep out the chill of the evening and wool rugs would be wrapped around the girls as well.

John lifted Mary up onto the cart and Jean jumped up nimbly beside her. William climbed onto the back after he had untied the horse and then they were off at a smart pace headed for the hall which was a short distance from the town of Clifton.

Soon the horse was tethered alongside several others and was munching on a nose bag full of grain. He had been given a drink from the water trough when they arrived and William would check on him from time to time during the evening.

Mary smiled up at John as she took his arm. "That was a very nice picnic. We will have to do that more often."

"I agree, my dear. Nothing would please me more that to be with you every day." John squeezed her arm as they went into the foyer of the hall and took off their coats to hand to the attendant. John paid the entry money for the group and they went inside. Nick Postles was looking out and came over to join them. He was soon whirling Jean around in a lively dance.

John and Mary set off in a more dignified manner while William joined the younger lads who congregated at the back of the hall. The evening continued in a most convivial manner with Nick claiming Jean a number of times and escorting her to the supper room.

John suspected that William and his friends had a quantity of liquor hidden somewhere outside the hall as they disappeared at frequent intervals. He smiled indulgently, as he remembered doing the same thing when he was their age.

The evening finished with the singing of 'Auld Lang Syne', a traditional Scottish song of farewell written by Robbie Burns, and then it was time for the revellers to untether their horses and head to their homes.

****

Once again, John Cameron had avoided telling Mary about his plans. He had already written to the timber mill and accepted the position and once he made his steamer bookings they would refund his fare. A job would be waiting for him when he arrived and a cabin reserved for him. There was a central cook house where meals were provided, but John knew that conditions were basic and there would be no home comforts.

The opportunity to inform Mary came about unexpectedly. The Gregg family had driven to town to pick up some supplies and Elias had business to attend to at the bank, when Mary appeared at the salon. John had just finished cleaning the bath house after a customer and was taken aback to see her standing there.

"Do come in, my dear. This is an unexpected pleasure for sure." He ushered her up the stairs and she sat down on the lumpy couch and looked around.

He had planned to make the steamer booking for two weeks' time and knew he couldn't put off informing her any longer.

"I'm pleased you have called as I have some news which will come as a surprise to you. I'm planning on taking steps to make an early wedding possible, but unfortunately it involves moving to another town where well paid work is available."

Mary stared at John in disbelief. Perhaps he was planning on working in the nearby city. That would be ideal as she could get a job there as well.
"What sort of work are you considering and where would it be?"

John sat beside her and took her hand. "The work is in a small timber town in the North Island, but I only plan to go for a short time and make enough money for us to marry soon."

Mary's face turned pale. "The North Island is many miles from here. Are you sure there are no opportunities for well paid work in Dunedin?"

"The economy is bad at present and jobs are hard to come by. I could earn enough in a few months in Springvale to set us up financially and we would have a great future together."

Mary's eyes filled with tears. It was good news that John wanted an early marriage, but the thought of him going so far away filled her with apprehension. What if he forgot her and never returned?

John stood up and paced the room. This decision was more difficult than he had imagined. He hated hurting this sweet young girl who obviously loved him, but he knew it was for the best. Time would soon pass and they would be back together again.

He turned to face her. "I will call at your home tomorrow night and discuss the situation with your parents.

I'm sure they will understand my motives. I wouldn't like them to think I was abandoning you, my dear."

Mary gave him a watery smile. She knew that John would be back as soon as possible and they could plan a marriage in the near future. And if John wasn't close by, there was no reason why she couldn't take up the promised job with her aunt in Dunedin.

She stood up and took him in her arms. "I hate the thought of you being so far away, but if it means that we can be married sooner, then you have my blessing." John returned the hug and promised to see her the next evening when he would try to convince her parents that he was doing the right thing. He knew in his heart that they would understand.

****

Jason's friends were pleased to see Alana and welcomed her into their circle. Their Wellington team was playing away tonight and the group enjoyed a few drinks as they watched the match unfold on the big screen.

Alana was pleased to catch up with Carla once again. She knew that they could be good friends as they came from similar backgrounds. Carla's new job was going well and she was learning to navigate the streets of Wellington as she visited clients in their homes. Many of them had recently been released from hospital and need-ed help with mobility or access problems.

"Sometimes it's just a matter of a ramp or a door being removed to allow access," she said. "Others want us to transform their whole bathroom with all the latest gear."

Alana explained briefly about the completion of her project and that she would be looking for another job when they returned from their trip to Taupo.

Carla's boyfriend Aaron pricked up his ears when he heard this news. "What's going on here, Alana? You've got this man trapped I see." He laughed and pounded Jason on the back which made him spill the beer over his shirt.

"Thanks a lot Aaron. Just when I'm trying to be on my best behaviour."

Just at that moment, Pete and Sharon turned up and wanted to know what was going on. "I think our Jason's in love," Aaron persisted. "They're going on a honeymoon to Taupo."

"Leave them alone. Jason's doing fine and they don't need you making fun of them," Pete scolded, but punched Jason on the arm all the same. They all laughed and settled in to watch the second half of the game. The three girls chatted and shared the events of their week. Sharon worked as a nurse in a doctor's surgery which had recently become a group practice. "We now have eight doctors and several nurses and everyone is learning a new routine," she said.

Alana was envious that the two of them had such secure jobs. Her life was a roller coaster of uncertainty and she knew it was time to try to find permanent employment. She looked across at Jason and realised that she wouldn't want her work to take her too far away at this stage.

As soon as the match ended Alana found herself inviting the other four to her apartment for a coffee. After all, it was just five minutes up the road and they had all planned to catch a bus back to their dwellings later in the evening.

They climbed the narrow steps with great hilarity and with six people crammed into the living room the apartment did appear to be small and crowded. But everybody raved over the view and the location.

"This is gorgeous, Alana. I'd swap our flat for this any day."

After their friends had left, Alana and Jason curled up together on the Queen-size bed and fell into an exhausted sleep. They had a whole weekend ahead of them.

Chapter 28

The time for John's departure to Springvale came up all too quickly. There was a lot to be done to leave the business in Nick's hands and pack his belongings for the journey. Nick was to move into the rooms above the salon and run the bath house as well as the barber's shop, paying the lease of the whole building. He had given up trying to entice women into the salon and would concentrate on his male customers.

John had said his farewells to Mary the previous night and although she was sad to see him go she was in high spirits about her move to Dunedin. "I will be back as soon as I can and we will be married," John promised as he rode away, leaving Mary fighting back the tears.

He was to travel by coach to Dunedin the following morning and set off on the steamer to Wellington the next day. Although the timber company had reimbursed his fare, John had little left in the way of funding.

He gathered together some pens and paper as he hoped there would be an opportunity to do some writing while he was away. He would certainly correspond regularly with Mary and his mother and may have time to write some articles to sell.

On his last evening a few of his friends gathered at the hotel to wish him well. "You'll earn enough to buy the whole town, no doubt." Many of them were envious at the opportunity to make big money. It reminded them of the old days when gold fever had hit the region.

John looked around. He was sorry to be leaving the place he knew so well but knew it was the only way to provide a home for Mary.

The next day the coach ride took him through fertile farmland and then along the coast until they reached the city outskirts where he would stay overnight in a hotel room. He retired early as he had to board the steamer first thing in the morning, taking a horse-drawn cab to the wharf.

Once on board he was shown to a four-berth cabin as the journey was to take the best part of two days, calling at Lyttleton on the way. He stowed his gear onto the bunk and wandered out onto the deck to watch them depart.

Dunedin had grown into a bustling city with several majestic buildings and streets of smaller dwellings. Many of the passengers were attired in the latest fashions and there was a general air of prosperity among those headed for the first class accommodation.

The majority, however, were down at heel and shabby but there was a look of hope on their faces as they journeyed off to their new destinations.

As they steamed out through the gap in the harbour to the open sea, John headed into the lounge area and ordered a glass of beer from the bar. He found a table by a window and took in the mostly barren coast-line, with the occasional fishing settlement and stands of native bush.

A young man in a rough wool jacket joined him and they were soon in conversation.

"Where are you heading?" John asked and the man replied that he was going to Christchurch to work in a woollen mill close to the city.

"How about yourself?" he enquired. John told him of his job offer in Springvale and the man looked at him curiously.

"They're a rough crowd up there," he said. "You'll need a strong back to keep up with those mill workers, but they say the pay is good and you look as if you could tackle it."

John had removed his jacket and the young man had caught sight of his muscular arms.

"I certainly hope that my weight training will pay off. I'm willing to give anything a go just to secure a better future."

"Then good luck to you." The man moved away and John was left with his thoughts. After a simple meal and a few more drinks John decided to settle in for the night. Two of his cabin mates were already asleep on their bunks and John took off his shoes and jacket and lay on a bottom bunk. The man above him was snoring but the rhythm of the boat soon rocked John off to sleep and he was surprised to wake and see the faint light of dawn through the port hole.

After using the small washroom, he decided to go out and stretch his legs on the deck. They had docked at the Lyttleton wharf during the night and most of the loading and unloading of the ship had been carried out. The city of Christchurch was just over the Port Hills and several of the passengers had already disembarked.

John decided to find something to eat and returned to the lounge to find a table. Most were already taken but a group of men moved closer together and offered him a space. It seemed that they were all heading for the timber mill town on their arrival in Wellington.

"We will be able to share transport I am sure." One of the men shook John by the hand and introduced himself as Charlie. He spoke to the other men and they exchanged information about themselves. It seemed they all had a similar story of needing to receive a better wage than they could get in their home towns.

John was glad to hear that few of them had any logging experience and would have to learn on the job. At least they were all in the same boat and would survive by working together.

It was late afternoon when the hills of Wellington came into view. The steamer negotiated the narrow entrance and John could see rows of houses built on the steep slopes. The boat harbour was in the middle of a bay with narrow streets running up towards the hills.

After they had disembarked, the group of men stayed together and Charlie, who had assumed a leadership role, arranged for two carriages to take them to the settlement of Springvale early next morning.

John was glad to be in the company of these men who were all as anxious as he was to find out what lay ahead for them. But now they had a night to spend in the city of Wellington from where the country was governed. There were a number of small hotels and boarding houses close to the wharf so it didn't take long to find accommodation and then they agreed to meet at the nearest tavern for a meal and a few glasses of ale.

Some of the men were anxious to meet the 'ladies of the night' who hung out on the street corners down on the waterfront. John wasn't tempted as he thought of Mary waiting for him back in Clifton. Instead he walked along the jetty and past the boat sheds, admiring the elegant wooden homes situated around the bay.

There was scarcely any flat land in Wellington and he was amazed how the houses clung to the rock face, with steep paths and steps rising from the streets below. These were the homes of gentlemen he was sure, many of them involved in government work. Yes, it would be a grand place to live once he had made his fortune at the timber mill.

****

Another weekend had come and gone and Jason was once more on his way back to Springvale while Alana worked hard to finish her project. She planned to hand it in to the museum by Thursday and then she could relax and join Jason at the Springvale tavern. They would leave for Taupo on Saturday, calling at the farm for two nights and then continue on towards Napier.

 She had made an appointment with her doctor for Monday afternoon for a check up and to get contraceptive advice. Fortunately, their reckless love making hadn't resulted in a pregnancy but she knew it was time for her to take the initiative.

The grave listings were completed and printed out in a folder, but there was still work to be done on the history of Springvale and the timber industry in particular. Alana had pages of scrawled notes and rough photo copies to sort through. She would somehow weave the story of John Cameron into the work as an example of someone who was living there at the time.

She spent Monday morning at her keyboard, only stopping to text Jason and reply to his messages. The trip to the doctor's surgery took some time as she caught a bus into the centre of town and another connection to the suburb where the health centre was situated.

Her doctor was a young woman who checked her over and advised her on the brand of pill to use. She noticed that Alana appeared anxious when she asked about her job. "It must be difficult to maintain an apartment in Oriental Bay without a steady income," she commented.

Alana laughed and said it was hardly larger than a shoe box but she was keen to secure a more permanent job. The doctor agreed that living a 'gipsy' lifestyle could make you anxious and advised Alana to look at making a few changes. "I think your little holiday will be good for you," she said. "But try to sort out your employment status as soon as possible."

As Alana left the surgery she realised that she had been feeling a little tense lately. Her sleep was often interrupted with visions of John Cameron and the lonely grave in Springvale. So much was happening in a short time and she would be glad to finish this project and look for a more permanent job. It would be a relief to wrap up the Springvale assignment and enjoy the break away with Jason.

That night she fell into a troubled sleep. After several hours on the computer her mind was overloaded and the dreams were vivid. The shadowy figure of John Cameron kept cropping up in the most unexpected places. She visualised him walking along Oriental Parade and then he was sitting on a park bench beside a river.

He lay down on the bench and fell asleep and Alana tried to rouse him. She woke up with a jolt but couldn't shake the ghostly images from her mind. The sad figure was haunting her.

It was only four o'clock in the morning so she got up and warmed a cup of milk. She felt restless and walked around the apartment before settling back in bed with a paper back. Reading a light novel should take her mind off John Cameron.

Chapter 29

The first sight of Springvale was a welcome one as the weary travellers alighted from the carriages in the middle of a small village with one main street lined by wooden storefronts.

The horses were unharnessed and led away to the stables where they would be fed and watered while the men waited outside a small office building for someone from the timber mill to arrive.

Most of the men were to continue on to the mill where they would settle into their cabins while others had arranged for lodgings in the town. John set himself down on a sturdy wooden bench and looked around. It was almost like being back in Clifton except there were more hotels and lodging houses to cater for the timber workers.

The journey had been more convivial than he had imagined and he felt that he was already amongst friends. There had been a few light hearted moments on the journey and he had managed to make them laugh with his rendition of a rather bawdy ballad or two.

It wasn't long before a stout man appeared holding a clip board with a list of names. A few of the men had ducked into the nearest hotel for a quick pint but they soon came out and stood with the rest.

"Good afternoon gentlemen. I trust you had a good journey to Springvale. My name is Samuel Peters and I represent the Springvale Timber Company."

He explained that the carriage would leave for the mill in half an hour and advised the men to buy any provisions they would require during that time. "All your meals will be provided at the camp but you may want some personal items. You won't be back in town for at least a week," he warned.

John wasn't sure what he would need. He had packed soap and other toiletries but decided that some tobacco for his pipe and a bottle of whisky might be a good idea. He hurried off with the other men to pick up their supplies.

The journey to the mill took almost an hour by carriage along a track which followed the river. It was a rough clay road and John knew that when the rain came it would be almost impassable.

"This is proving to be quite an adventure," he said to Charlie, who was seated beside him. "It is all beginning to feel rather unreal."

"I'm sure reality will strike when we are handed an axe or a saw and set to work." Charlie was looking at the huge trees which towered above them on the side of the track.

Giant Totara, Matai and Rimu stood tall, saved from the fires which had razed most of the forest in the early pioneering days. While much of the land had been cleared for farming, many acres of native bush had been spared to be used to create the thriving timber industry.

The carriage rattled into a clearing and the expanse of the mill site came into view. A large wooden building beside the river dominated the scene and along the edges of the clearing, a row of small wooden huts could be seen.

"Home sweet home," said Charlie. "I guess this will be our lot for the next few months."

John was one of the first to jump down from the carriage. He claimed his luggage and looked around. There was the clang of machinery coming from the mill, which was powered by a giant water wheel set in the fast-flowing stream.

He headed for his allotted hut, number eight, eager to pack away his belongings. The door was ajar, sagging on its hinges. One small window lighted the dark interior and he saw that there was a simple bunk bed along one side and a rough wooden table and seat along the other. An oil lamp stood on the table and two grey blankets were folded on the end of the bed.

John threw his bag in a corner and looked around in dismay. He hoped the cook house offered a little more comfort than this. He drew out his bottle of whisky and took a sip, then he set about hanging his clothes on a row of hooks on the wall. A wash bowl stood on a wooden stand outside the door and a grimy towel hung over a rail.

Soon the men began to congregate in the yard and wandered around checking out the rest of the site. The cook house proved to be a large shed with long tables and bench seats. The smell of cooking was wafting from the row of stoves behind a counter where the food would be served.

"Something smells good." John and the others were hungry and realised that they hadn't eaten since breakfast. One of the mill workers came out to welcome them. He pointed to a large urn on the counter and a row of tin mugs. "Help yourself to a mug of tea or if you prefer, a warm beer," he said. The men couldn't believe their ears. A mug of beer would go down well right now. They hadn't realised that this would be part of their food allowance, thanks to the proximity of the excellent brewery.

They settled down at one of the long tables and it wasn't long before the mill workers came drifting in, weary from the hard day's work. They had washed their hands and faces, but their clothes were grimy from sweat and saw dust.

Several of the workers came over to welcome the new recruits and although they were tired, there was plenty of cheerful banter. Soon John joined the line of workers at the counter and carried a plate of meat, potato, pumpkin, spinach and gravy over to a table.

It looked as though they would eat well and as he poured another mug of beer, his spirits rose. Maybe Springvale wouldn't be too bad after all.

****

After working on her assignment for two full days, Alana was relieved to be able to take the finished product into the maritime museum and hand it to Estelle Jones.

"Thank you my dear. I'm really looking forward to reading it," she said, as they sat enjoying a coffee in the restaurant at the rear of the building.

"I'm pleased to be able to take a break and then I will have to start seriously looking for a new job." Alana felt a huge sense of relief at finishing the project. She walked around the city that afternoon with a new spring in her step and had arranged to have a meal with her friend Angela who she had neglected recently.

Several end of season sales caught her attention and Alana couldn't resist a new sweater and a smart pair of trousers to take on her holiday with Jason. She knew she would have to watch her bank balance carefully from now on but needed a couple of new items to freshen up her wardrobe.

Angela was waiting at the Thai restaurant when she arrived and they were soon catching up on the latest news over a glass of wine.

"When am I going to meet this Jason?" Angela asked. "I'm dying to check him out."

"We will definitely have to get together soon," Alana promised. "It's been hectic living between here and Springvale and we are heading off on Saturday."

They agreed to have a meal together when Alana and Jason returned. Angela didn't have a current boy friend and Alana wasn't sure how she would fit in with Jason's friends. Rugby and beer were definitely not Angela's style.

They enjoyed their chicken and noodles then Alana returned to pack ready to travel to Springvale the next morning. She missed Jason when they were apart and was looking forward to being with him for 10 whole days. Text messages were fine but not quite the same as being together.

Thursday morning turned out cool and cloudy and the drive to Springvale was a pleasant one. Alana's first call was at the tavern where she was given a key to Jason's room where she left her luggage and then she carried a folder of papers to the museum where Flo Avery would be waiting for her.

Flo was excited. She had called at Norman Todd's garage and offered to take the boxes of papers off his hands. "I told him I would sort through them and keep any important documents safe. I feel that there is a huge amount of important information amongst Emily Todd's notes."

"I want a break from John Cameron for a while, but if you come across any new information let me know when we get back from our holiday." All Alana wanted to do was sit around and read a book.

However, without the pressure of working on her project she soon felt restless and decided to drive out to the old timber mill site to catch up with Jason. She picked up some filled rolls and drinks from the café and set off along the road beside the river.

When she arrived at the clearing, Alana was relieved to see Jason's vehicle parked beside the road. She followed a track through the fern and scrub until she came to the old mill site. Remnants of the water wheel could still be seen beside the stream and the foundations of the mill stood out like monuments to an earlier time.

There was no sign of Jason so she tried to find evidence of the row of cabins which had housed the workers. The bush had taken over but an occasional patch of broken concrete took her eye.

It was hard to imagine that this deserted place had once housed a bustling timber industry employing several hundred men. A number of Totara and Rimu trees had regenerated over the years, but most of the regrowth was Manuka and tree fern interspersed with clumps of pampas grass.

But now she could hear a rustle in the bushes and the crunch of footsteps on the gravel track. Jason strode into view and when he saw Alana he hurried towards her.

"Hey, fancy seeing you here. I was just about to grab some lunch so come and share it with me." Jason had brought along a pack of sandwiches from the tavern and a large slice of Jan Evans' chocolate cake.

He took Alana by the arm and led her back to where the vehicles were parked. They found a sheltered place where the grass was smooth and sat down on a blanket to enjoy an impromptu picnic. Alana knew that her vacation had well and truly begun.

Chapter 30

It was difficult to sleep on the narrow bunk bed but next morning John felt ready for the day ahead. The new employees were to assemble after breakfast and they would find out whether they were to work in the mill or the forest. John would have preferred to be out in the open but instead found himself directed into the mill where he was to feed lengths of milled timber onto a belt which took them out to a waiting cart.

Even with his weight training the work was hard and the boards were heavy. He paused at times and wiped the sweat from his brow. After a few hours the sound of a whistle brought everyone to a halt and after washing in a drum of water the men paraded into the cook house for a welcome cup of tea.

"How are you surviving?" One of the workers asked, and John admitted that the work was hard but he thought he would manage.

"You seem to be doing fine from what I could see. It gets easier as time goes on."

Then it was back to work until the lunch break which was a little longer. Soup and bread was served and the afternoon shift began. Around four o'clock the manager came around and instructed the new hands to finish work for the day. "We don't want you wearing yourselves out the first day. Freshen up and come back for a beer before dinner."

The men wearily returned to their quarters and John threw himself down onto his bunk. He had never worked so hard in all his life, even when he had helped out on the farm. After a short time he dragged himself to his feet and took a large tin jug to the water tank. He poured the water into the bowl beside the door and stripped to the waist. The cold water felt good on his tired muscles and pulling on a clean shirt he made his way to the cook house to join the other workers.

Charlie was already pouring himself a mug of ale and John followed suit. Beer was only available for a short time each day, after work and during dinner, and it had never tasted so good. "Here's to our first day. We survived that so I think we will be okay." They sat down on a bench outside the cook house and watched the other workers return from the forest. Many of them had spent all day on the end of a cross saw but they were accustomed to the work.

Soon it was time for the meal to be served and once again John piled his plate with a tasty meal, this time it was stew, potatoes and beans, followed by a piece of apple pie.

He refilled his mug with beer and found space at a table. The men were all friendly and included him in their midst. After dinner he sat down at his crude table and began a letter to Mary. It wasn't long, however, before his eyes grew heavy and he lay down on his bunk and was soon asleep.

****

Alana spent the rest of the afternoon with Jason who was wrapping up the job at the mill site. They were able to get away early and returned to the tavern where Jason showered and dressed ready for the evening ahead. It was too early for a meal so they walked hand in hand down to the bank of the stream and rested on a bench in the park.

In a clump of bushes a short distance from the path Alana noticed the remnants of an old seat. She went over to take a closer look and pulled aside the branches. Three short posts remained and a broken board covered with mould.

"This must have been here for a while. Maybe since the timber mill days." She was about to call Jason over to take a look but at that moment she saw a figure sitting on the bench. He wore a coat and hat and his head was in his hands.

She gasped in surprise and looked again but the figure had gone. Trembling with fright she ran back to Jason who looked at her in astonishment. "You look as though you've seen a ghost," he said.

"I think I just did. Come on, let's get out of here. This place is giving me the creeps."

Alana clutched Jason on the arm and pulled him away from the park. She shivered, but didn't tell Jason what she had seen. She definitely had been working too hard and it was just as well they were taking a break.

They walked through the village and came to the pizza restaurant. "Let me buy you a beer," Alana said and guided Jason up to the bar. She felt like a long drink and ordered a gin and tonic with ice and lemon for herself and a beer for Jason.

"Here's to our holiday," she said and raised her glass. Jason had some paper work to complete next morning and then they would be free to get away. There was no reason for them to delay their journey so they decided to leave Springvale sometime next morning and head back to Wellington.

Later that night it seemed strange to be sharing Jason's room and Alana felt shy undressing in front of him. Their love making was uninhibited, however, although Jason still used a condom as Alana wasn't sure how long it took for the pill to be effective.

"The doctor said about seven days but I want to be certain," she said.

While Jason was finishing his work next morning, Alana walked along the street but avoided the graveyard. She didn't want to risk any more ghostly apparitions. After dreaming about the park bench and then imagining a figure sitting there she had a bad feeling about it. John Cameron had died of exposure. Perhaps the bench was where he had died.

She called at the museum to say goodbye to Flo, who was reading the copy of Alana's assignment. "This will be a welcome addition to our collection," she said. "I like the way you have written a short history of the timber industry and interwoven a little about the life of John Cameron. The cemetery list too will be invaluable for family researchers."

It was around 11 o'clock when Jason and Alana finally left Springvale. Jason led the way and they stopped at a seaside settlement just outside Wellington for lunch.

The plan was for Alana to call and pick up her bag and then drive to Jason's house in the Hutt Valley. They would set off early next morning, driving Alana's small car which was more comfortable than Jason's utility and head for Alana's brother's home near Taupo.

****

With the bags stowed away and a road map handy, Jason and Alana set off on the long trip north. Their journey took them through a number of central North Island towns, mostly serving vast farming areas, then over steep country until they reached the desert road in the centre of the island. From here they could see the majestic mountain peaks of Tongariro National Park and then the huge expanse of Lake Taupo.

Jason had driven most of the way and Alana took over, driving through the town of Taupo and then out to the western side of the lake where the family farm was situated.

She had texted her brother before they left Taupo and knew that they would receive a warm welcome when they arrived. As they drove through the familiar gates and onto the graveled driveway, a large black and white cattle dog ran alongside barking loudly.

"That's old Tip. He doesn't do much work but he's been around for ever." Alana was happy to see her old friend. By the time they pulled up outside the garage, Sandy and Joanne were there to meet them.

Sandy was tall and dark and looked a lot like Alana. His wife Joanne was small and fair with a friendly smiling face. "Hi stranger. It's good to see you." There were hugs all round and the bags were hauled from the car and carried inside where they were left in the hallway of the spacious farmhouse.

Soon they were all sitting around the kitchen table while Joanne brewed a pot of tea and produced a plate of homemade biscuits. "Our mother has been telling us all about your graveyard project. She thinks it sounds rather melancholy," Sandy laughed. "I think she's a little worried about what you will be doing next."

Alana looked serious for a moment, then smiled. "I'll worry about that next week when we get back to Wellington, but now I just want to enjoy this holiday."

Jason was soon busy explaining a little about his work and how they had met at the tavern. "It was my lucky day when I accidentally sat at Alana's table, and I'm very happy to meet her family."

At that moment, Sandy and Joanne looked at each other. "We have some good news to share as well. We're going to have a baby." They held hands and smiled into each other's eyes. "We have only just told Mother and believe me, she is over the moon."

Alana jumped up and threw her arms around her sister-in-law. "That's great news. I'm so pleased for you. Just think. I'm going to be an aunt." She smiled at Jason and took his hand.

Jason shook Sandy's hand and added his congratulations. "Good one," he said.

In high spirits, they sat around the table enjoying the tea and catching up on all the news. "I've left it up to you to choose a room," Joanne said when they had finished. "The beds are all made up and you will see that we have added a new bathroom onto the guest bedroom."

This was a surprise to Alana. Several of the rooms had been painted in warm colours with new drapes and bed covers and the extra bathroom was a pleasant surprise. "We'll use the new guest room," she decided. "We may as well start this holiday the way we plan to continue."

The girls laughed as Alana carried the bags into the stylish bedroom while the two men disappeared outside to look at the new tractor. "The dairy pay out was very good last year so we were able to upgrade a few things.

It's been a bit too dry this season so it may not be quite as profitable, but I guess you have to take the bad with the good."

They checked out the small bedroom beside the master suite which had been painted in pastel shades ready for the new arrival. Joanne was already in her fourth month but after a previous miscarriage, she had kept it from the family until she knew the pregnancy was secure. She showed Alana the photo of the scan and they laughed at the long legs and the finger in the baby's mouth.

"I like the look of your new man. He's a keeper." Joanne gave Alana a hug. "I have a feeling you will be very happy."

Alana agreed. "Yes, I'm very lucky to have met such a fabulous person. We get along really well." They admired the small pile of baby clothes lying on top of the dresser and Alana felt a stab of envy. Maybe her biological clock was trying to tell her something, but having a child was not on the agenda just yet.

Chapter 31

John Cameron's first week at the Springvale timber mill seemed to go on forever. Each day was the same, loading timber onto a conveyer belt in the dusty noisy building. When Saturday came the men worked until lunch time and then headed for the hot showers and a change of clothes before they were taken by horse and dray into the village.

John discovered that it was also possible to travel in a small boat down the stream into the town and he might look at that option some time in the future. He had written a letter to Mary describing his week and was eager to post it while he was in Springvale.

He had chosen to receive a small allowance from the mill and the rest of his wages were paid into a bank account in his name. There was little opportunity to spend money at the camp although some of the men liked to play cards in the evenings. But that held little interest for John. As long as he had some tobacco for his pipe and a bottle of whisky he knew he would survive.

He wished he had his horse here to ride into town but there would be nowhere to graze it. He waited for the first cart to return and was lucky enough to find space on the second trip. The track was rough but the horses were strong and made good time and soon John arrived at the settlement. First he walked down to the edge of town and found himself in a small park beside the stream. Ducks swam on a lake and a number of benches had been built around the edges of the park.

He sat down on one of the seats and took in the scenery. It was a welcome change from the bustling atmosphere at the mill site. He thought about Mary and wondered how her job was going in Dunedin. Perhaps there would be a letter waiting for him at the postal agency.

With that on his mind he walked back in the direction of the town and passed the hotel where he had enjoyed a drink on his arrival in Springvale. The Imperial Hotel was the largest in the village, and the most imposing with its wooden verandahs and impressive balustrades.

He would have a quick drink here and then search for the postal agency. The bar was already full to overflowing and Charlie beckoned to him from the other side of the room. "Come and enjoy some great hospitality. The beer is cool and the food great."

John ordered a glass of the finest ale and a sandwich and sat back in comfort. A week at the mill site certainly made you realise what you were missing. This village was so much like being back in Clifton, except that his family and his beloved Mary were far away.

He bought another pint of beer and wandered across the room to where a piano stood on a small stage. He sat down and played around with the keys until a young man walked up and took over the seat. "What do you like to sing?" he asked and John named a popular ballad of the time. The young man began playing and John sang along. There was silence in the crowded bar and then some of the patrons joined in. They were singing along with John Cameron and applauded him when the song was over.

Someone brought him another beer and he sang again. Then he realised that he had not called at the postal agency so he excused himself and walked along the street until he found the store where mail was distributed. He paid for his letter to be sent to Mary then waited for the clerk to find any mail addressed to him. He had almost given up hope when the young man appeared brandishing two letters, one from Mary and one from his mother Margaret.

John walked out onto the street and saw that a horse and dray were ready to return to the mill site. Most of the men were still relaxing in the hotels but he was keen to return to his humble cabin and catch up with the news from home. He had eaten little, but had bought the tobacco and whisky so he was ready to leave.

Back in the cabin he lit the lantern and sat on the hard bench to open his mail. He read the letter from his mother first. It was full of news of the farm and life back in Clifton. They all hoped he was coping with the work and looked forward to his return.

John lay back on his bunk as he opened the letter from Mary. He moved the lantern closer so he could read the contents.

"Dearest John, I miss you so much but hope you are doing well in Springvale. I travelled to Dunedin on Monday and am staying with my aunt who owns the store where I will be working. If only you had found employment in this city everything would be perfect.

"Today I started work in the haberdashery store and was overwhelmed by the range of fine products on sale. I am working in an area that specialises in fabrics and trimmings and have learned to measure out the material and fold it into a tidy parcel.

"I hope your accommodation is comfortable and wish you well in your first week at the mill. I can't wait to see you and once again be in your arms.

"I love you, Mary."

John couldn't believe that he was here in this dreary little hut when the rest of his family was living in comfort. Mary had no concept of the conditions he was enduring. Fine fabric and tidy parcels indeed. She was living in a different world and he almost resented it.
There was no work at the mill on the morrow as it was Sunday so he would rest and work on his writing. There was nothing else to do in this God forsaken place.

****

Alana and Jason had an enjoyable evening with Sandy and Joanne. Alana phoned her mother and they were invited to lunch at her town house the next day. There would be time to visit the hot pools first as well as the amazing spectacle of Huka Falls where the turquoise water foamed down to the river below.

After the long drive, Alana and Jason were ready to retire early and the gorgeous guest bedroom was waiting. They enjoyed a shower and then sunk into the luxurious Queen size bed where they kissed good night and fell into an exhausted sleep

Jason was up early next morning to accompany Sandy as he rode his four wheeler around the farm, driving the cattle to fresh pasture and checking the water troughs. Alana stayed in the comfortable bed as long as possible then reluctantly got up and joined Joanne in the kitchen.

As soon as the boys returned, Joanne cooked a country breakfast with bacon, eggs and hash browns which was soon devoured along with tea, coffee and slices of toast spread with home-made marmalade.

"I never eat this much at breakfast. I guess being on holiday has given me an appetite." Alana refilled her coffee mug and sat back in her chair. "But we need to get going soon if we are to visit the hot pools and the falls. I want to give Jason the guided tour."

They left Sandy and Joanne to carry on with their chores and headed off back into Taupo and along the road to the popular hot springs. As they walked down the path through the native bush they could smell the sulphur and see the steam rising from the ground.

They paid their admission fee and disappeared into the changing rooms, to emerge minutes later in their bathing suits. The baths were warm and relaxing with several pools at differing temperatures. Cascades of water fell from a rock and bubbling springs close to the edges provided a vigorous massage.

"This is my first time in a mineral pool," Jason confessed. Alana found that hard to believe as she had been coming here since she was a young child. "It's so relaxing, but it doesn't pay to stay in too long," she warned.

An hour later they were back on the road and heading for the Huka Falls, where the sight of the foaming water roaring towards the water fall attracted tourists from all over the world. There were several mini buses and campervans already in the car park and as they crossed the bridge and looked down at the torrent below, they could hear a number of different languages.

Although Alana had visited the falls many times she was always amazed at the sight of the bright turquoise water foaming over the rocks. From the lookout they could see a jet boat carrying passengers to the base of the falls far below. Jason took out his camera and photographed Alana several times and she laughingly took the camera from him and aimed it in his direction.

A young Japanese couple asked Alana to take their photograph and then took a photo of the two of them, the falls cascading behind them. "Our first photo together," said Jason. "We'll have to treasure that one."

Back at the car, Alana combed her hair and touched up her lip gloss. "I'd better look respectable for my mother. She will think I've been in the country too long.'

Jason was feeling nervous. Margaret Cooper sounded like a bit of a dragon, but when they pulled up in the driveway of the plush townhouse she came out to welcome them, her face wreathed in a smile. She gave Alana a quick peck on the cheek and took Jason's hand. "I've been dying to meet you. Do come in and talk to my friend Frank. He will be pleased to have male company while I catch up with my daughter."

They followed Margaret into the house which had been carefully furnished in the latest colours of cream and beige. Vivid red pottery and candles provided a contrast and the glass topped table held an assortment of delicate sandwiches and Oriental savouries.

"My goodness. You really have gone upmarket. A bit different from the scones and jam back on the farm." Alana couldn't help teasing her mother who took it all in her stride.

"Come and meet my dear friend Frank. He and I belong to the same Bridge club right here in Taupo." Frank was sitting on the couch but stood up as they entered and held out his hand with a crooked grin.

"Alana, at last we meet. I already know your brother and his delightful wife." Frank was of medium height, a little overweight with a round, pleasant face. "Good to meet you, Jason. I hope your trip up here was an interesting one. I believe this is new territory for you."

The men chatted for a few moments while Alana followed her mother into the kitchen which was separated from the dining area by a long breakfast bar. Margaret warmed up some tiny bacon and egg pies and placed them on the table. "I think this calls for a celebratory drink," she said. "Would you like to do the honours, Frank?" A bottle of chilled sparkling white wine was produced which Frank poured into slender crystal glasses.

The bubbles hit Alana on the nose and she giggled. Trust her mother to turn this into a party. She really seemed to be enjoying town life which was great and Frank looked like a nice, dependable person. They sat down and sampled the food which was as delicious as it looked. The conversation flowed and the next two hours passed very pleasantly indeed.

Chapter 32

As the next few weeks went by John Cameron grew more despondent. Each Saturday he received a letter from Mary but she seemed to have no idea of the conditions he was working and living under.

"I think Mary visualises me in a quaint little cabin in the woods chopping up firewood," he said bitterly to Charlie one evening. "I'm doing this just for her, but she doesn't seem to realise how difficult it is."

Charlie was sympathetic. He was worried about John who seemed to be sinking into a low frame of mind. The only bright moments came when they spent the afternoon in Springvale drinking and singing around the piano.

John was also having trouble with his chest which was aggravated by the dust from the mill. It wasn't so bad when he worked outside loading the timber onto the wagon but when he had to work indoors the only thing that soothed his cough was an occasional sip of whisky from the flask in his pocket.

They were enjoying a beer at the Imperial late one afternoon when one of the workers came up to John and told him that he was returning home and that his room at the boarding house would be vacant.

"You'd be paying some of your hard earned wages but I tell you, it is worth it," he said.

John knew that with winter approaching he couldn't stay much longer in the cold, draughty cabin so he gave the idea some serious thought. His wages were mounting up and he knew that he could afford to pay the rent for the room.

"I've heard that Mrs Todd is a very good landlady and provides a hearty meal as well," he said. "Please put in a good word for me and I will call and see the woman next time I am in town."

The only disadvantage to living in the village was the carriage ride to the mill which meant an early start, but the luxury of a comfortable bed and warm surroundings would more than make up for it.

He was in a cheerful mood for the rest of the week and the following Saturday he called at the lodging house in Grange Street to meet Mrs Emily Todd. She was pleased to see him as she had heard that he was a gentleman and would be a suitable tenant for one of the small rooms attached to the back of the house.

She had invested in the large house and she had space for 10 boarders who all had their own sleeping quarters but shared the bathroom and living areas. Meals were served in the kitchen close to the warm stove.

John looked around and couldn't believe his luck. If he moved into this comfortable accommodation it would take longer to save for the marriage, but he was tired of being the one to make such a big sacrifice.

"I would dearly love to take a room here. It reminds me of my family home back in Clifton." Emily Todd liked what she saw and agreed that he could move in the following week.

Once again he joined the men at the Imperial and sang alongside the pianist. He bought no beer as he was kept supplied and by the time they left for the mill settlement he had to be helped onto the cart by his friends.

****

Alana and Jason's holiday was a great success. From Taupo they moved on to Napier and spent several days checking out the shops, museums and galleries and walking on the beaches. They visited the area's orchards and vineyards and lunched at a popular winery right beside the ocean where they sampled the best of the vintage wines.

They stayed in a quaint motel close to the waterfront and each night they lay in each other's arms. After a few days, Alana decide that it was safe to rely on the pill, so Jason cast aside his protection and their love making brought them closer than ever.

But all too soon it was time to return to the city. Jason was to start back at work on Monday and Alana needed to look for a new job. She didn't want to go back to her lonely apartment and Jason was equally loathe to return to his Hutt Valley dwelling. As they approached the outskirts of Wellington Jason looked across at Alana and told her he wanted them to move in together.

"What's the point of us having two houses when we could live in one?"

Alana was thrilled. She knew she wanted to be with Jason for ever but where should they go? Her flat was too small and Jason's too far away from the city for her liking.

"Okay. Let's start looking for something that would suit us both. But I really need to find a job as soon as possible."

Jason dropped Alana off and picked up his vehicle. It was a sad moment as they wanted to stay together, but they knew there was plenty of time for that. In the meantime, they agreed that Alana would join him in Springvale later in the week.

****

When Alana woke next morning there was a message on her phone from the maritime museum. "Please call and see us. There could be work here for you." She dressed and went down the steps to the nearby café where she picked up a coffee and a muffin then headed along the waterfront to the museum.

She was a little early and sat on a bench watching the activity on the wharves until the doors of the museum opened. Jonathan Wilson was already in his office and welcomed Alana like an old friend.

"We were very pleased with your research and would like to have you on our staff. One of our girls is off on maternity leave from next week and could be away at least six months."

Alana felt like hugging Mr Wilson but restrained herself and listened patiently to the rest of news. It seemed that she would be supervising the primary schools programme which involved organising the school visits, preparing work sheets for the pupils and speaking to the groups.

It wasn't exactly the type of work she was trained for, but would provide much needed employment for the next few months.

"Yes please. That sounds great and I'm free to start work next week." She spent the next hour with Chloe, the woman who she was replacing, and knew that the job was within her scope. Mixing with excited groups of youngsters was just what she needed right now.

Two bookings had been made for later that day, so Alana went off for a coffee and returned to help Chloe and observe her in action. Chloe guided the children around the exhibits and pointed out the main features. There were question sheets to be filled in as they went around. It was full on but fun.

Back at the apartment, Alana texted Jason with the good news. He replied almost immediately. "You'll be great!"

Now, the next thing to do was to find accommodation large enough to share, but close to the city. Alana checked the website but was horrified at the cost of central city apartments and most had little or no parking.

Maybe they could manage in her small apartment for a while as she could walk to her new job from there. She was so excited about working at the museum and already had ideas for a new work sheet for the children based on some of the questions they had asked.

Alana decided to contact Angela and tell her the good news. She would buy in some food and they could have a meal together before she left for Springvale on Thursday.

****

John was only just tolerating the work at the timber mill, spending as much time as possible outdoors away from the dust, loading the carts with the milled boards. Some would be used to build houses and the sturdier posts were used for the framework. Most nights he lined up for a hot shower and then joined the other workers for a couple of beers and dinner.

He didn't relish going back to the cramped little cabin and had dragged a seat outside where he sat and wrote letters when the weather allowed. Winter was almost here and the evenings were getting shorter so the location beside the river was always cool and damp.

Early on Saturday morning he packed his few belongings ready to take the carriage into Springvale that afternoon. It would be a huge relief to move to the comfort of the boarding house.

He shared lunch with his new friends who were envious of his good fortune and then it was time to leave for the village. Emily Todd welcomed him and showed him into his room, which was just large enough for a bed, a dresser, a small round table and a comfortable chair. He hung his coats and shirts in the corner cupboard and packed the rest of his clothes into the drawers. This was luxury indeed!

Mrs Todd offered to throw his dirty laundry into the boiling copper and this was much appreciated. John Cameron was beginning to feel almost human again.

He celebrated at the Imperial and the requests for his songs came thick and fast. He was careful not to drink too much as he didn't want to make a bad impression on his new landlady the very first night.

After a delicious meal of roast beef and Yorkshire pudding John retired to his room and wrote a cheerful letter to his mother and another to Mary. He had called at the postal agency and collected his mail which kept him in touch with life back in Clifton where they had experienced an early snow fall.

Tomorrow he planned to rest for most of the day and take a walk beside the lake during the afternoon. For the first time in a while he wished that Mary was with him to share a picnic in the park. It would be good to have her arms around him and feel her warm body close to his but knew he would have to be patient a little longer.

Chapter 33

Thursday turned out to be wet and windy and Alana drove slowly out of the city towards Springvale. She had spent several hours at the museum, assisting Chloe with the school groups and learning about the programme ready to begin work the following week.

"I'm so glad that you are able to take over," Chloe said, as she was leaving. Her due date was two months away and she was more than ready to take a break.

"It's just come at the right time for me. It'll be a welcome change from studying grave sites." Alana knew that she would enjoy her new role and was anxious to get started.

She was surprised to find Jason in his room when she arrived at the tavern. He was catching up on some book work as it was too wet to work out on the road.

They ate lunch together in the dining room where Alana shared the news of her job offer with Jan and Bruce. "Sounds like you got a lucky break. Good for you."

The weather cleared up during the afternoon so Jason drove back to the new site while Alana read a book and checked the news on her computer. It was a good chance to take a break before starting work next week.

After an hour she was ready for a walk so she set off through the town and along Grange Street past the old boarding house. The park was at the end of the road but she was loathe to go there in case she had another encounter with the ghostly figure on the bench. She retraced her steps and decided to call at the Springvale Museum to share her news with Flo Avery.

"I was just thinking about you. I found some more notes in Emily Todd's account books that might be of interest." The books were piled on Flo's table in the office and she had marked a number of pages to discuss with Alana. "It looks as though John Cameron was at the boarding house for about two months and then something must have happened to him."

"I know he died at the end of August so that would be about right." Alana didn't think she was learning anything new.

"The last reference I can find about your Mr Cameron is at the beginning of September when Emily Todd has let the room out to a new boarder."

"Mr McDonald in poor John's room. Took money owing for rent and sent his belongings back to Clifton. Hope Mary gets the bank book. She will need it for the baby."

Alana gave a gasp of surprise. "That is really terrible. So, Mary was pregnant and hopefully she received John's earnings, but the poor girl never got to marry her fiancé." Alana felt sad for the young woman who had waited in vain for her loved one to return. "I'm almost wishing I had never started this search. Even 100 years later the story is getting quite depressing."

"You're right. There are probably many sad stories to be found in that grave yard. But it seems as though your own life has taken a turn for the better."

When Jason returned from work, Alana clung to him as she told him the latest news of John Cameron and Mary. "It sure is a sad story," he agreed. "But our life's good right now and it's time to enjoy a drink before dinner."

Alana smiled. After four days apart it was great to be together again.

****

A week after John Cameron had left for the North Island, Mary Gregg was in the city of Dunedin and already working at the haberdashery store which was owned by her Aunt Marjorie.

Marjorie had never married and ran a very successful establishment, selling all manner of clothing, materials and everything necessary for sewing a garment. There was also a separate department which sold bed linen and towels.

It was in the dressmaking department that Mary found herself on the second day. Measuring out the lengths of material and trimmings was a constant pleasure and she was able to choose just the right shade of thread to match the cloth. Her aunt was happy with her work. She also boarded with her in the spacious home set on a hill overlooking the town.

Mary's life was so busy she scarcely had time to think of poor John working in the timber mill so far way from home. In fact, after a month she could hardly remember what he looked like and found it difficult to correspond with any real feeling.

When his letters arrived she felt a tinge of guilt and wrote back straight away, but the rest of the time she felt as though they were living in different worlds. A young man working in the next building had invited her to walk with him and she was tempted for a moment. But she looked down at the pretty little ring on her finger and reluctantly shook her head. Perhaps she had been too hasty in agreeing to this marriage.

By the second month she was considering writing to John and calling off the engagement. Maybe he was feeling the same way and regretting his promises. But then something happened to change her mind. It was actually something that didn't happen when her monthly bleed failed to appear.

Mary was devastated. She kept the secret to herself but a month later when nothing happened again she knew that she would have to let someone know. She was feeling well enough and not suffering from the sickness which afflicted many women, but her breasts were tender and her stomach starting to swell.

"You are doing so well in your work I am thinking of letting you run your own department," Aunt Marjorie confided in her one evening. Mary burst into tears and her aunt looked at her with concern.

"Is everything all right my dear? I trust that you are happy living here with me."

Mary had to tell someone about her predicament and she sobbed as she told her aunt what had happened. "Then you must write to John Cameron and let him know this instant. He must return and marry you as soon as possible. Now dry your eyes and go and write the letter."

Mary felt relieved that she had shared her news and even felt a tingle of excitement that she might be married to John much sooner than she thought. She folded her hands over her stomach and thought about the baby inside. Perhaps John would be happy that they were to have a child.

She got out the writing paper and began the letter. She screwed it up several times before she was happy with the result. Yes, her aunt was right. John must come back and marry her and the sooner that happened, the better it would be.

****

When they returned to Wellington for the weekend, Jason stayed the night at Alana's flat and they decided that it would be possible for both of them to live there as long as he didn't bring too much of his gear with him. There was space in the garage for a few boxes and just enough room for Jason's utility on the parking strip beside the driveway. Alana's car fitted in the garage and would hardly be used as she could walk to the museum. Of course, for the next month, Jason would be gone all week until his roading project was completed.

Alana was able to pack away some of her belongings to make room for Jason's gear which they would bring over during the weekend, along with a small cabinet for his clothes and his cassette player. He would need to give notice to his landlord but was sure another tenant would be found easily.

They were in high spirits as they walked across to the boat shed to meet their friends. Alana was enjoying their company more each week and realised that she had been quite lonely before she met Jason.

Everyone was pleased to hear that Alana had a new job to go to the following week and they decided to eat out at the Irish pub in Courtney Place to celebrate. Alana hadn't been there for some time and laughed as they crowded into one of the alcoves and sat around the roughly sawn table.

"I'm giving up my unit next week and moving in with Alana." Jason was happy to share their news. "I think it will be great being a city slicker for a while." He endured the usual teasing in a good humoured way.

The pub was crowded and after their meal they wandered along the street passing several more eating places all brimming with night life. "There's nothing like Wellington on a Friday night," they agreed.

Saturday proved to be a busy day as Alana helped Jason clean his unit and pack his belongings onto the back of the utility. He didn't own the furniture so they were able to stow most of his gear into boxes. Two book cases and the small cabinet would fit easily into Alana's apartment.

Jason said goodbye to the neighbours, left the key with the real estate office and they were on their way. They planned to call his father later in the day and let him know his change of address. He had lived in a retirement home in Christchurch since the death of his wife several years before and Jason's only brother lived close by.

"We must visit them soon. I haven't been very good at keeping in touch."

The rest of the day was spent rearranging the apartment and although it was even more cluttered than before they knew that they would cope. "We can start looking for something bigger when I have finished at Springvale," Jason promised.

Chapter 34

Although the work left him exhausted, John Cameron was much happier now that he was living in Emily Todd's boarding house. The other men proved to be good companions and after dinner they would often spend time at the Imperial where John's songs continued to be popular.

"You could take this up as a career. You don't have to spend your life working at a timber mill," the pianist often told him.

"That would be a great life but there would be little money in it," John answered. He knew that he had managed to save a considerable sum and was hoping to leave Springvale soon and travel back to Clifton. He was sure he would find work there and he and Mary could be married.

Sometimes when he thought about Mary doubts sprang into his mind. Although he wrote to her every week, days could go by without any thought of her. Her letters were full of her work and the latest fashions and it was hard to tell whether she was missing him. If he returned to Clifton he would be able to get back in touch with his feelings and have a better idea of the strength of their relationship.

His landlady Emily Todd was a fine woman, a little older than himself but still attractive in a calm, dignified way. She often sought him out for a conversation and fussed about his cough which had improved since moving into town.

"Working in that dusty mill is doing you no good at all," she would say. "You are making too much of a sacrifice for your young lady."

He occasionally shared stories of his life with this woman and she told him of the tragic loss of her husband leaving her with a young family to raise. "That's when I opened the house to guests," she explained.

When Mary's latest letter arrived he took it to his room and sat down on the chair to read it in comfort. It was just as well he did as when he read her news he almost fell over with the shock. Surely she wasn't carrying his child. Although they had twice lain together he couldn't believe that a baby had resulted.

"You must come back and marry me as soon as possible," he read. How could he support a wife and a child? He shuddered at the thought and put the letter down on the table. Then he picked it up again and carried it out to show Emily.

"You must do the right thing and marry the girl," she said. "I'd be sorry to see you go but you really have no choice." She patted him on the arm, then hastily drew away.

John felt a lead weight in his gut. What would her family say? The thought of facing Elias filled him with dread. He went back to his room and began aimlessly packing a few of his belongings into a box. The thought of returning to Clifton was whirling around in his head.

He took a sip of whisky and sat down to reply to Mary's letter. He told her he loved her and was proud to think that he would soon be a father. They would marry when he returned and find somewhere suitable to live. He did not put down his true feelings, but signed the letter and put it aside in case he had a change of heart.

He fell asleep that night dreaming of a woman but he could not see her face. Next morning he left early for work, his mind still in a turmoil. When he returned with the other men that evening he didn't go to his lodgings but went straight to the Imperial where he ordered a large whisky.

It was a night like any other. After a hard day at the mill what else was there to do? The liquor flowed and the crowd was boisterous. They urged him to sing their favourite songs from the homeland and filled his glass over and over.

But then it was time to be sent out onto the road. Time to go, but John was not ready to return to his lonely room just yet. He staggered off in the direction of the park at the end of the road where he sat on his favourite bench, a solitary figure with the moonlight shining down on his slender frame.

He pulled the whisky flask from his pocket and took a sip. He coughed and took another mouthful. His thoughts returned to Mary and the expected child. In his befuddled state he tried to work out what he would do. Of course he wanted the beautiful Mary, and the child would be most welcome.

"Mary, my dear, we'll be together soon." He said the words aloud and they sounded good to his ears. He coughed again and pulled his coat around him more tightly. He drained the flask and closed his eyes to dream of better things and then he fell asleep, the winter air closing in around him.

They found him the next morning but the doctor could do nothing to save him. The effects of the alcohol and the freezing temperature were too much for his tired lungs.

His funeral was arranged hastily as they had no record of a next of kin to call. His name, age and cause of death were filled out by the doctor, along with the date, 30 August, 1912.

Emily Todd was one of the first to be informed of the sudden death of John Cameron. Next day she joined the few mourners at his graveside and blinking back the tears, threw a single red rose onto the coffin as it was lowered into the ground.

When she returned to the boarding house she lost no time in packing his belongings carefully away in a large box. She took the money owing to her from a bundle of notes in a drawer and parcelled up the rest of the money, along with a few letters and a bank book and addressed it to Mary Gregg. The parcel was placed inside the box and sent off to Main Street, Clifton, the last known address for John Cameron.

Next day the room was let out to a Mr McDonald who also came from Otago in the South Island and was there to start work at the timber mill.

****

In spite of the chilly wind and a chance of rain, Alana happily walked the length of the waterfront for her first day at work. She had only one group arriving today which would be good practice for the rest of the week. Jason had returned to Springvale the night before but his belongings were still littered around the apartment.

It wasn't long before the seven and eight-year-olds converged on the museum. Alana welcomed them and began showing them around the most interesting exhibits. Some of their questions took her by surprise.

Their comprehension of the past was totally different from her own.

They filled in their question sheets before they left and Alana collected them to analyse their answers. She would have fun making up the new work sheets which she was sure they would enjoy.

The apartment seemed empty without Jason and she began picking up his clothes and folding them into the drawers. Friday night was a long way off and now that she was working regular hours she wouldn't be able to travel to Springvale to join him. Hopefully his next job wouldn't take him away from home during the week.

Although her assignment was finished Alana's thoughts kept returning to the sad story of John Cameron. What had become of Mary and the child? She pulled out the rough notes she had made and flicked through them several times before piling them into a box and shutting them away in the hall cupboard.

To clear her mind, she walked along the waterfront past the sandy beach in the middle of the bay and sat for a time looking up at the stately villas on the hillside above the band rotunda. She knew these houses would all have stories to tell, some happy and some sad.

During the week she continued to read the real estate pages in the newspaper and on the Internet. She asked the other museum workers whether they knew of any affordable apartments close to the city.

"I really think Jason and I will be falling over each other in my small place. It's not really fair that so much of his stuff is stored in the garage." Her workmates were sympathetic. There were a large number of inner city apartments available but parking two cars would be a problem.

"Why don't you try one of the suburbs on the train line? The railway station is close to the museum and the trains run frequently."

Alana thought this was a good idea and began searching for rental properties on the Johnsonville line. She and Jason could check them out in the weekend.

****

Nick Postles was having a quiet day back in Clifton when he was surprised to find a large box left in the salon addressed to John Cameron. He thought he should open it as he wasn't sure when John would be back. He was still seeing young Jean Gregg from time to time but had not been in contact with her sister Mary since she had left for work in Dunedin.

He was puzzled when he found John's clothes folded neatly along with a bundle of papers and a package of letters. Perhaps he was on his way back and his belongings had arrived before him.

He looked again at the parcel and saw it was addressed to Mary Gregg. He would keep the box safe until John returned. Yes, that would be the best thing to do.

When a week went by and there was still no sign of John Cameron he began to worry. He knew where John's mother lived and decided to ride out to the farm and enquire about any news of her son. She greeted him warmly when he arrived and invited him inside for some refreshments. Margaret Cameron wanted to hear how the salon was going and whether Nick had made any changes to the business.

She then prepared a tray of tea and biscuits and they sat in the warm kitchen near the stove. "We haven't lit the fire in the sitting room. We prefer to spend most of our time in here," she explained.

They sat for a while and Margaret asked Nick whether he had received any correspondence from John lately. "It is strange that he hasn't written to us for several weeks. His letters were always more frequent."

For some reason, Nick was loathe to tell her about the box of clothes and papers. He would look inside the package when he returned and see whether there was any indication of when John would return.

As soon as he returned to the salon he pulled out the box and studied the contents. He noticed John's favourite pipe lying beside the package and that made him even more concerned.

He didn't like to open the parcel without someone else there so he called out to his butcher friend and asked him to come into the salon. "What do you think about this, Joe? Would John Cameron ever be parted from that pipe?"

Joe agreed that it was very strange and they opened the pile of papers. Most of it was hand written notes about events at the mill and a few crumpled newspapers. There were no answers to their questions there.

"I don't like to open the parcel addressed to Mary. What do you think we should do?"

"Perhaps we should contact Mary's father. He is a good man and would know what to do." The two men felt uneasy. They hoped there was a good reason for John's belongings to be returned.

Nick was kept busy for the next two days and it wasn't until Saturday that he found the time to ride out to the Greggs' farm and talk to Elias. Young Jean was happy to see him but he was anxious to speak to Elias alone so told them he had business to discuss.

"What can I do for you, young man?" Elias asked. "Is it something about my daughter Jean?" He hoped that Nick was not wanting to walk out with his younger daughter. He was still concerned about the engagement of Mary to John Cameron.

"No sir, nothing like that. It's just that I have received a box containing John Cameron's belongings, but there has been no sign of the man himself. There is a package in the box addressed to your daughter and I thought I should tell you about it."

Elias looked puzzled. He wondered whether his daughter had received a letter from John over the past few days that might solve the mystery. He could telegraph her but that would surely upset her if she didn't have any information. Even if he contacted the timber mill at Springvale it would be many days before an answer was received.

Elias poured two brandies and the men sat and considered the next move. They would wait a few more days to see whether there was any word from John and in the mean time Elias would contact the timber mill and wait for a reply.

Chapter 35

By the time Friday came, Alana had gathered a list of prospective properties within a short commute to the city, so on Saturday morning they set off armed with the addresses.

If they saw a property that appealed they would contact the agent and get more details. They drove through the hills as far as Johnsonville at the end of the line and found the three properties on the list. "We might just as well stayed on in my unit," Jason said. "This is just about as far out of town."

They moved on to the next suburb, but nothing caught their eye. The available houses were tucked away in a shabby area with no outlook and several young children playing on the street.

Eventually they arrive at Khandallah, a leafy suburb with views over the harbour. "This is more like it," said Alana, "but I guess the rents will be too high here." Jason had been thinking. He had saved enough to put a deposit down on a house, and between them they would probably manage the repayments. It could work out cheaper than paying rent.

He noticed a real estate office in a small shopping centre and stopped the car. "Let's see what they have available here." The window was full of photographs showing a wide range of properties, some new but mostly bungalows and villas. Alana's eyes grew wide. "Do you really think we could afford something like this?" she asked. A young woman came to the door and asked them what they had in mind.

She pulled out a list of options arranged in order of price. It was soon obvious that most of the properties were very expensive and there were only half a dozen in a lower price range.

"Most of these are small units or town houses but this one is rather nice." She pointed out an old cottage with a garden full of trees. "It needs a bit of a tidy up but the house is sound and in an excellent street."

Alana and Jason looked at each other. It sounded promising and the repayments would work out cheaper than a rental. Wasting no time, the agent closed the office, and they jumped into her car and drove up the road and around a few corners. When they stopped outside the address they were not disappointed. The cottage was small but the kitchen and bathroom had been upgraded and there was a glassed in sun porch along the side.

They looked at each other. It was exactly what they were searching for. The interior was dark as the shades were drawn but when Alana looked out the lounge window she could see the harbour and the hills of Wellington in the distance. "I know I could live here," she said, and Jason agreed. It wouldn't take much to brighten the place up and it was just a short train ride from the city. There was space for two cars in a carport at the side of the house and a wooden deck out the back was perfect for a barbecue.

"Give us the weekend to think about it," Jason said. "But I'm sure we would be able to raise the money." They returned to the office and were given the details and promised to get back to the agent on Monday morning.

Back in the car, Alana gave Jason a big hug. "This would be a perfect place to live," she said. "I know we would be very happy here."

****

Back in Dunedin Mary was beginning to panic. She hadn't received a letter from John for three weeks, ever since she had told him of the expected child. Perhaps he was going to abandon her.

Her aunt could see that she was unhappy and thought it was time to speak to her parents. She wrote to Mary's mother saying that they were worried that they hadn't heard anything from John, but she did not mention the pregnancy. She wanted that news to come from Mary herself.

When they received the letter Elias decided that he should journey to Dunedin and speak to his daughter. "I will take the package for Mary to open," he said. His wife agreed that it was the only thing to do. "There might be something in the package that will tell us what has happened to John." She packed a bag for Elias and sent him on his way.

Mary was surprised to see her father when she came home from work that evening. She wondered whether her aunt had told him of her pregnant state but he said nothing about it as he sat down beside her on the couch and handed her the package from John.

"We're very worried that no-one has heard from your fiancé and this package arrived a few days ago addressed to you," he explained. He handed the bundle to Mary who accepted it with shaking hands. Surely John hadn't gone away and not let her know.

She undid the string and slowly opened the package. A pile of letters fell out onto the table followed by a bank book and a bundle of notes. Elias looked on in amazement. There was a tidy sum and even more according to the bank book. John Cameron had done very well indeed in the short time he had been in Springvale.

Mary was anxiously searching through the letters. Most were notes that she had written to John, the most recent one at the bottom of the pile. She gasped as she noticed an envelope with her name on it. It was unsealed and for some reason John had not posted it.

The tears fell down her cheeks as she read the words of love and the promise to come home and marry her.

"What is it? What is wrong?" Elias asked. "Is there news of John in that letter?"

Mary shook her head and hugged the letter to her breast. "He says he is coming home to marry me but why hasn't he returned?" Aunt Marjorie was standing in the doorway looking on anxiously. "I think you should tell your father of your condition," she said. "We can't hide the problem any longer especially when we don't know what has happened to John."

Elias looked closely at his daughter. He took in the bonny face and the rounded figure and knew at once what was upsetting Mary. If she was with child it was even more important to locate John Cameron.

"My dear, it will be alright. We will take care of you." He gave her a quick hug then sat awkwardly back on the couch. He was not used to showing any emotion and he wished that his wife was here to handle the situation.

After reading the letter from John, Mary clutched it and lay back in a chair, her face pale and her eyes red from weeping. She tried to cling on to the hope that he would keep his promise and come back to marry her.

Elias stayed in Dunedin overnight and returned to Clifton on the next day's coach. He would have to break the news to his wife and it was imperative that John was found. He had received no reply from the timber company and decided to visit John's mother and discuss the situation with her. Perhaps she would know of the whereabouts of her son.

****

Alana was so excited about the little house in Khandallah that she hardly slept. She had no groups booked for the day so she called the museum and asked for time off to finalise the purchase of the cottage.

As soon as the bank opened, Jason and Alana were in the door and wanting to see a loans officer. They had all the details of the property with them and found that with the deposit he could put down, Jason could finance the purchase himself. Alana would of course contribute towards the expenses.

They left the bank hand in hand and returned to the car. The next stop was the real estate office where they were able to sign the agreement. Everything was happening so quickly that Alana felt as though she was caught up in a whirlwind.

As they left the office, Jason took Alana's hand and said: "I have something I want to ask you. Will you marry me?"

Alana's head was spinning. She would need to come down to earth some time but at the moment felt as though she was on another planet. Marriage was such a nice old fashioned relationship but she knew that Jason craved security. "She gave him a huge hug and whispered in his ear. "I think I might consider it," she said.

They drove back to Wellington in a daze. Alana was due back at work but Jason decided not to return to Springvale until the next day. There was so much to celebrate tonight.

****

After her father's visit, Mary wasn't well enough to go to work for several days. She received a letter from her mother saying that she should come home until they received news of John. She decided, however, that she would be better off working in the store as it would take her mind off her problem.

Elias and Mary intended to call at the Cameron farm but as it turned out, Margaret and her daughters called at their home first. They were increasingly anxious about the absence of correspondence from John and were keen to know whether the Greggs had received any news.

When Elias broke the news of receiving his belongings they weren't sure what to think. Perhaps he had left for Australia as many young men did. Leaving the girls in the sitting room with Elias, Margaret and Mary busied themselves in the kitchen making tea and buttering scones.

"There is something else you should know but it's confidential at this stage. Our Mary is with child and out of her mind with worry. She is afraid that John has deserted her. Do you think your son would be likely to abandon his responsibilities?"

"It doesn't sound like my son, but you never know. Perhaps he panicked when he heard the news and didn't think he could provide for a wife and child." Margaret was concerned at her son's behaviour but patted Mary on the shoulder and assured her that they would help in any way they could.

"There is a child to think about. We will have to do our best to help your daughter through this trying time."

"Elias and I think it would be best if Mary and I confine ourselves to the house once her condition is noticeable. If John fails to return Elias and I will bring the child up as our own and Mary's reputation will remain unblemished."

Margaret knew that there would be speculation and rumours about the parentage of the child, but agreed that it would be for the best. The secret would be safe with her.

"Of course, we will all hang on to the hope that John has been delayed and will return to marry Mary." But both women knew in their hearts that this was not to be.

Before Elias and Mary returned to their home they decided to stop off in the village to pick up some supplies and check for messages at the postal agency. Sure enough, a telegram had arrived the day before and when Elias read it his face was grim.

"Sorry to inform you that John Cameron died of pneumonia following exposure and was buried in the local cemetery. Please accept our condolences. Springvale Timber Company."

Epilogue

It was a beautiful day in late spring when Alana and Jason were married. They had decided on a small family wedding and after a simple service in a picturesque old church beside the lake at Taupo, the guests all converged on a winery just outside town for the reception.

Alana wore an elegant white gown, while her bridesmaid Angela wore a rose coloured silk dress. They both carried a bouquet of pink roses and trailing fern. Jason and his best man Pete were resplendent in their hired grey suits complete with a silver waistcoat.

They had restricted their guests to mostly family with Jason's father and brother travelling the longest distance to be there. Four of their friends from Wellington had also been invited as well as Bruce and Jan from the Springvale Tavern who had taken a rare weekend off to join the celebrations. Alana's mother was at her charming best, dressed in an ensemble of violet silk and escorted by her friend Frank. Sandy and Joanne were enjoying the day and showing off their newborn son who slept peacefully in his carry seat.

"This is such a happy day. I can't believe that we only met because of the graveyard project, and maybe the ghost of John Cameron brought us together." Alana laughed at the thought.

"We would probably have met eventually at the boat shed. After all, we must have been so close on several occasions. I'm sure we were always meant for each other." Jason felt very content. He had found the love of his life and would honour her for ever.

They spent the night in a lodge overlooking the lake and next day set off back to Wellington and their charming cottage which was being lovingly renovated. Then they were booked to spend 10 days cruising the islands of the Pacific, taking time off to enjoy the perfect honeymoon.

But now they were on the road heading for Springvale. There was one more thing they wanted to do. They pulled up at the cemetery where Alana had spent so many hours. Jason opened the back of the car and pulled out a plain wooden cross. They walked towards the familiar grassy mound and dug a hole to loosen the earth.

Jason took a hammer and banged the cross into the ground, then they stood back and said a silent prayer for the man who was buried there. The small brass plaque gleamed in the sunlight and the words stood out for everyone to see.

John Stirling Cameron.
1877-1912 R.I.P.

9 780473 253394